Maksim Haretski

TWO SOULS

TRANSLATED FROM THE BELARUSIAN
BY OLYA IANOVSKAIA

Grunwald Publishing
P.O. 405
Minden, Ontario
Canada
K0M 2K0
grunwald.ca

First edition July 2024
Second edition September 2024

ISBN 978-1-7383142-0-1
ISBN (e-book) 978-1-7383142-1-8

FOREWORD

First published during the Russian Revolution in 1919, Two Souls explores the complexities of identity, social conflict, and national consciousness in early 20th-century Belarus. Set against the backdrop of the revolutionary period and the struggles for Belarusian independence, the novel follows the life of Ignat Abdziralovich, an officer who is searching for love, but is forced to navigate numerous personal and societal upheavals instead.

Two Souls was written by Maksim Haretski, who is known as the first Belarusian existentialist writer. The book's philosophical depth and vivid storytelling offer a profound commentary on the human condition and the conflicts between collective and personal aspirations.

Two Souls is recognized for its courageous critique of the Socialist Revolution and Bolshevism, which led to the novel's suppression for many years. Despite this, the novel had a significant influence on Belarusian philosophy and literature: an early 20th-century Belarusian philosopher Ignat Kancheuski published his seminal essay on Belarusian philosophy, borrowing the name of the book's protagonist, Ignat Abdziralovich, as a pseudonym.

The present translation was undertaken with meticulous effort to retain the original flow and linguistic style of the novel. Every effort was made to stay as true to the original as possible, ensuring that the nuances and depth of Maksim Haretski's work are preserved for English-speaking readers.

The Publisher

I

A moderately wealthy landowner, Mr. Abdziralovich, became widowed rather tragically in 1890.

On a stifling, dark summer night, he and his wife were returning home from a ball where the nobility from the entire district had been reveling.

The celebration was grand. Champagne flowed like a river. Noise, chatter, and the rumble of the orchestra brought in from N. echoed from the brightly lit manor house, flowing through the old silent park planted by the hands of the subjects of King Poniatowski, flying across the overgrown lake with its rustling canes and whispering reeds, rolling, while gradually fading through the sleepy fruit orchard, and dissipating over the courtyards of the slumbering village.

Amid the general unrestrained merriment and dancing, under the cover of night and music, a young, anxious lady suddenly felt an inexplicable sadness, thereby greatly alarming her husband. She urgently insisted on going home, where their firstborn, three-month-old Ignalik, had been left.

"But, dear," protested her husband, rising from the card table, trying to dispel the premonition of misfortune. "It's still so early... All is calm... We've gathered a good party here..."

The lady suddenly shivered all over. Tears sprang from her eyes and burned his hand where they fell.

"My Ignalik... Ignalik... We must get home quickly to him..."

The ball-goers didn't pay much heed to the strange anxiety and concern of the young wife, and continued their revelries until the gray of dawn, when the peasants, grabbing their scythes, rushed through the foggy haze toward the hayfield, faintly hearing the diminishing sounds of the festivities as they went.

The foreboding did not deceive her: amid the black darkness, at the Devil's Bend, around midnight, a group of vicious highwaymen brazenly attacked them and vanished without a trace.

The horses slowly and cautiously stepped over the rutted forest path, twitching their ears and snorting with apprehension. The phaeton[1] jolted and creaked. Trembling uncontrollably, the lady clung to her husband.

Something cracked, something rustled... And right nearby in the woods, by the road, someone called out, seized the horses by the reins, and struck the carriage for the first time, sending a strange echo through the muted silence of the forest and piercing it.

The second time they aimed at the master but struck his wife in the temple instead.

The horses reared and dashed away like mad. In a terrible frenzy, the distraught master roared like a beast and gripped the lifeless, cooling body with his blood-soaked fingers. The

---

1. A phaeton is a type of an open carriage drawn by one or two horses; it was popular in late eighteenth and early nineteenth centuries.

coachman froze with fear, desperately holding on by his legs so as not to fall off the box and tear off his hands, which had the reins wrapped around them.

Disgruntled and restless, sleepy birds rustled their wings among the branches, unseen in the darkness.

Ignalik was left a frail orphan. Numbed by grief and rage at the suspected murderers, whom he believed to be the neighboring peasants, Mr. Abdziralovich shut himself in his study with cognac and cigars, seemingly forgetting about the existence of his child.

Loyal servants procured a wet nurse from a distant village, and with her, her baby boy, a lad almost the same age as the young master.

A makeshift cradle was set up in the nursery, hastily constructed by the estate carpenter and rather unappealing against the beautiful cradle of the young master. Yet, both babies were almost indistinguishable, and both were entirely in the care of the nurse.

"Eat, drink, don't worry about anything!" the master once said to the nurse. "I only ask you one favor: treat the children equally when you feed and care for them."

Having said this, he shut himself back in the study.

Malannya was a quiet, reserved, but sensible and compassionate woman, the wife of a man conscripted into the army and soon thereafter deceased, and she easily adjusted to her new life.

The boys were raised well. Ignalik found his footing, strong and handsome. Malannya's son Vasilyok was a little weaker and quieter.

The children were friends; they played together, grew up like brothers, listened to Malannya's fairy tales, and did not want to part when a respected tutor in a long black coat and glasses was brought to the manor to teach the young master literacy.

The nurse loved her foster child deeply. It seemed she loved him more than her own son.

Strange rumors began to spread in the distant village, but fortunately, none reached the master's ears.

He was proud of Ignas, sensing in him his own white bone and blue blood, his own lineage.

Just once, a peculiar moment occurred, when it seemed to Malannya that the master looked too long and too intently at Ignalik and then at the large portrait on the wall, where he was painted alongside his deceased wife.

Had he wanted to, Vasilyok could have easily become the master's own lackey, a cook, or even a steward, but his mother, as if intentionally, distanced him from herself, and once he turned seven, the boy ran errands for old Yaroma and tended the sheep.

When seeing him, Malannya would give him tasty treats from the master's table but remained strict. She did not like it if he came into the master's house too often and preferred to meet him in the servants' hut or at old Yaroma's cabin behind the orchard in the fields.

II

The train was delayed entering Moscow, and Warrant Officer Ignat Abdziralovich was pleased to arrive in the morning rather than at night.

He even regretted having to leave the cozy compartment.

The night had passed so well. There were just the two of them, in a first-class compartment, which he was allowed to occupy as a sick man; below, there was a reserved, nobly bred guards officer, and above, on the sleeping bunk, he, "an army warrant officer."

The train sped through the quiet July night. Out of the open window, distant, sparse stars glittered from the black, dense, and warm abyss. Outside and below, hills and hollows all rushed backward as if attempting to escape, with wheat clinging to the earth and with fragrant grasses; dark poles moved, remaining in sight, linked by the wire that flowed slowly upwards, then suddenly dove down, and again, first slowly, then abruptly re-emerged with a deadly glimmer from the light in the window.

With an air of self-importance, Abdziralovich's unsociable companion removed his travel bag from the net, carefully unlocked it, took out parcels of food, spread them on the table, pulled out a bottle and a glass, disregarding the cool glance from the neighbor on the upper bunk, and began to devour a large piece of roasted piglet, crunching on the golden skin; he then had some game meat, cheesecakes, and hand pies. He took his time peeling a huge, beautiful pear and smacked his lips, biting off large, juicy chunks.

Abdziralovich rustled the newspaper that reeked of fresh printer's ink and lay motionless for a while with his arms stretched along his body and with his ambiguous thoughts swirling.

The guardsman wiped his red, soft, plump mouth - a small, black mole visible over his clean-shaven upper lip - with a handkerchief that bore large initials underneath a crown. Then he wiped his chubby, well-groomed hands with a hand towel, and began to put everything back into the bag.

Abdziralovich had a wolfish appetite while recovering from his illness, and he now struggled with it in vain, swallowing saliva, sensing a certain dislike for the guardsman, because he himself could not eat like this.

He lit a cigarette and leaned out the window to savor the pleasant coolness of the night breeze.

After a month of severe illness in the divisional hospital, after the suffering and anxiety at his post, where the spirit of his earlier, younger self appeared to delight, after the tedious monotony of the checkpoints and railway stations, and doctors' commissions, he looked out onto the sleepy field with joy and a carefree feeling of lightness and peace in his revived body, breathing in the scent of hay and flowers. It seemed to him that he was being reborn to life again... Memories of distant years of his youth swirled, like when he had once run away from the courtyard into the field to observe the mowing of hay, when he had dined with the mowers, and rolled around in the fresh fragrant hay, and ran barefoot across the prickly hayfield.

Oh, how these thoughts and this pleasant night among the fields, aboard the rumbling train, atop the soft, bouncy pillows, oh, how they again stirred the heart that had emerged from the earth and was eternally drawn back to it, captivated by it and calling out to it amid the foreign and the unwanted.

The guardsman took out a small blanket and a pillow, rang for the attendant, and, with his help, carefully took off his shiny, polished boots. Then, having dismissed him, he undressed, neatly folded his French coat, removed its fur, lay down, tucked himself in, and fell asleep with a slight whistle in his nose.

The train thundered over the bridges, wheezed slowly uphill, raced over level ground among scattered black clusters of huts and gardens, where here and there windows sparkled with quiet, yellow village light. Far away, he could hear dogs barking from various parts of an unknown Russian village.

He daydreamed about working in a free country, about meaningful pursuits...

Everything seemed good now, everything appeared clear, and inexplicably understandable.

Even the image of his harsh, unjust father, who had disowned the people-loving simpleton and was glad that he had been expelled from the university; even he did not seem hurtful to him now.

And, looking at the well-fed, curvy guardsman, he recalled with sadness the battle sector of his company in Palesse,[1] among the forests and swamps... The company dwindled. Scurvy and dysentery reduced their ranks so fast! And oh, that time, when, in the spring, former gendarmes and personnel officers from reserve battalions overwhelmed the company... And oh, that time, when *velikarosy*[2] beat Captain N., a Ukrainian separatist... And oh, that time, when, insincerely, he had to persuade his people to patiently endure this abhorrent life...

He sensed bitterness and felt himself blushing, but only sighed lightly and calmly.

I'm getting better, he told himself, leaning away from the window and putting down his gray, coarse, but treasured overcoat instead of a pillow. *Getting better!*

In the morning, approaching Moscow, he awoke at peace with himself and content with everything around him and his fate.

The clouds walked across the sky; a fine rainy drizzle fell and smoked by the blackened factory chimneys, occasionally growing heavier and thicker.

I arrived in the rain: it's good luck, he thought to himself.

---

1. Palesse (also spelled Polesia, Polesie, Polesye) is a vast area of marshland and forests in Eastern Europe, stretching across the southern part of Belarus, as well as parts of Ukraine, Poland, and Russia. Palesse is known for its unique natural landscapes, which include some of the largest wetlands and peat bogs in Europe.

2. Velikarosy, *bel. велікаросы* – Russians.

While descending the steps down to the platform, he noticed and sensed that his legs stepped more firmly, no longer trembling the way they had back there, where the Red Cross aidmen had helped him onto the train.

The din and chaos of the station splashed over him.

Porters ran, heavily pushing huge carts of boxes, bundles, and baskets. City women, the likes of whom he hadn't seen in a long time, tapped their tiny feet.

Quiet and content with himself, he watched them, rejoicing that he no longer felt that old sensation - one that started so sweetly and beautifully but concealed emptiness and longing.

At the buffet, he pushed his way to a table through travelers and piles of things, and asked for a strong, black coffee.

He noticed a small, bright face with sparkling black eyes and unruly strands of hair opposite him, and calmly and easily averted his eyes, still pale, light, and pure after his illness. He could sense the joyful, cheerful, quiet laughter of the girl's sparkling eyes upon himself. But he didn't look up and was glad that he had become new and different.

On the noisy, wet, crowded, and chaotic street, he waited a long time and in vain among angry and annoyed people. He let several full trams pass, but remained patiently calm. He looked around with curiosity to see if there was anything new now, during the time of freedom, out on the city streets.

Everything was alright, everything agreed with him. Although he could not afford to hire a carriage and had very little money, he - who had experienced all the delights of a proletarian life after quarreling with his father - now wore an officer's coat, and while many of those around him may not have thought him an enemy, they did not accept him as their brother, either.

III

Nearly two months passed in Moscow, in the hospital, in grim anticipation of the transfer to the Caucasus for treatment.

Nearly all the officers had relatives in the city, nearly all were more or less healthy (he, as a recently commissioned officer, was being sent to the front), and they hardly stayed in the hospital, coming there only for lunch, dinner, and occasionally for overnight stays. Meanwhile, he would wake up and gaze out the window at the empty street, at the janitor in a white coat with a broom in his hands, and at the sparse, exhausted night coachmen, who were sluggishly heading homeward.

He found this solitude to his liking.

Only the flies were a constant annoyance, and Abdziralovich would retreat to a small garden pavilion entwined with wild grapevines to either read a book or just bask in the sun. His ill body hindered deep thought, leaving him with only a vague feeling: the raging revolution was passing by, just out of reach...

He was feeling considerably better; his stomach was no longer in pain, he no longer fainted, and felt reasonably good. Occasionally, in the evenings, he would venture out to listen to music or sit in the park square or walk among people – all while taking solace in his newly found freedom and independence.

Time passed, it got colder, and the sounds and colors of the approaching autumn were creeping into the city. The flies became less numerous, but they bit just as painfully and clung like resin.

His turn for a transfer would not come, and longing for the elusive stung his heart like a snake's fang, frightening him.

Around the table, officers would grumble about the crassness of the common folk; under the pretence of politeness, as though in jest but with real anger in their hearts, they would argue about politics with their *comrade waitress*, who delivered meals to the table, or chastised the meek and quiet refugee, *comrade medical assistant*, who did not even understand why they disliked him.

He risked succumbing to nerve-wracking stress again. *I need to leave here soon, soon*, Abdziralovich thought while sitting in the park square, watching passersby.

A worker strolled past, he was wearing a greasy blue blouse under a dilapidated overcoat without epaulets and drew attention with his strangely familiar appearance.

"Vasil!" Abdziralovich called out impulsively, and the worker stopped, recognizing him.

"Ignat Vosipavich?!" he uttered with timid joy, unsure whether to shake hands or not.

"Yes, yes, dear Vasilyok, it's me! How unexpectedly wonderful to meet you here in foreign Moscow!" and he embraced him simply and sincerely. They kissed.

"Vasilyok, it's as though you are ashamed of me," Abdziralovich said. "What's wrong, my dear? Come sit, my brother. Let's chat. Now, it's not like before – remember how they didn't let you, of lower rank, into the first-class auditorium with me in Smalensk?"

"Yes," Vasil replied evasively, eventually hitting the right note of reminiscence. But he, too, was pleased.

"Are you no longer a soldier?" Abdziralovich asked.

"No, I was discharged from the unit, and now I work at a factory. I live with Mother."

"What? Mother is here too!" he exclaimed, unsure how to speak of her, feeling ashamed to call her *Malanka* as before. "Oh, how great it would be to see her. Is she healthy, still strong as before?"

"Oh, there is no health, Ignat Vosipavich, only illness, with everything being so expensive. If she at least had better food."

They fell silent for a moment.

"If you don't mind..." Vasil said with a shy faint smile. "Come, the old woman will be so happy. She speaks of you every day. She tried hard to find out your address. Was worried whether you had been killed."

"Meanwhile, I, shamelessly, never wrote to my mother. Let's go, let's go... Ah, how wonderful. Trust me, Vasil, I'm as glad to see you as my own brother. I have almost nothing in common with my father. You probably know. And I have no one else. Though I've met different people. Ah, I don't want to think back to it. I am all alone again..."

They got up and headed for the tram. Both were happy. Excitedly and out of order, they told one another about events of recent years. The warrant officer barely recognized the Vasil of the old days, the carefree, cheerful, clumsy shepherd, and afterward a mill labourer. Now, he saw a serious, thoughtful, and slightly gloomy worker, who contemplated the significance of events and was an ardent supporter of the nearby social revolution. The officer even blushed a few times, embarrassed at his own ignorance and narrow view of the bloody struggle.

They rode for almost a full hour to an unfamiliar part of the city. Then for a long time, they walked along dirty streets, barricaded between enormous, unattractive houses, among factory chimneys, and along a very high fence.

"I like it. It's close to the factory for me," Vasil boasted.

They turned into a narrow alley, walked up into a huge courtyard, which reeked of tar and lime from pitifully constructed wooden outhouses, and finally found themselves in front of a low entrance into a cellar.

Vasil knocked.

"Our palace," he said.

"Who's there? You, Vasilka?" Abdziralovich heard the dear, familiar voice of his nurse.

"It's me, Mama, I... with a guest. Open up."

The doors that were patched with old rags creaked open, and she appeared at the threshold, looking very old, holding a candle stub in her hand.

"Please be so kind!" Vasil let the guest in first.

"It's alright, nothing to be afraid of, sir," she said with curiosity in her eyes, inviting him in while securing the candle stub into the bottom of a broken bottle.

"Don't you recognize me, Mama?" Abdziralovich stretched out his hands.

"Who are you, sir?" she paused and squinted. "Ah!" she suddenly squeaked and rushed toward him.

"Our little Master! Ignalik! Oh, Ignalik..." She grabbed his sleeve.

Tears ran down her wrinkled face; she was flustered.

"Hello, Mother," he hurried to embrace her, worried she might kiss his hand, as was customary at the manor, and kissed her gently.

"Oh, young Master! Ignalik... Forgive me for calling you Ignalik like when you were little. We are free now," she added shyly, completely at a loss, not knowing how to receive him, or where to seat him.

"Of course, of course. Mother, you can even tug my ear and say: *Ah, you naughty Ignalik, never wrote.* But believe me, Mother, life just happened this way. I didn't even know the address."

Vasil silently tinkered with the samovar pipe and, grabbing the handbasket that was black from coal, vanished through the door.

"I'm unhappy here. I would fly out of here if only I had wings, if it wasn't for Vasilyok," she looked around. "Oh, God, how could I? Forgot all about the samovar. I hadn't put it on, thinking that Vasil would spend the night at his committees. He's a Bolshevik — oh, a Bolshevik. And God knows what will become of all this... He probably went to Karpavich for coal. That one is also pulling for the Bolsheviks, even more so. Confuses our boy; they always argue and it gets heated."

The room was large but oppressive, with its gloomy, chilly walls and low stone ceiling with peeling paint. A single bed stood behind a curtain, and another one by the stove. A herring lay on a blue paper on the table. Several newspapers, brochures, and a thick book with a nice cover lay on a shelf by the tall, grated window. Abdziralovich lowered his head and read the embossing: "Capital."

Is Vasil really reading Marx? he thought to himself.

Meanwhile, Vasil returned with coal. The old lady bustled about with the herring, asking questions.

"Oh, our dear Lord, our Father," she said. "How the world keeps spinning year after year. Freedom has come, and still there is no end in sight. Our Karpavich is even angrier now. He only knows how to confuse the boy. Oh, if it weren't for the price hikes, maybe the people would soften."

They were eating the herring and drinking tea with cowberry extract when someone knocked at the door.

"Vasilyok! Ah, Vasilyok," a coarse but pleasant male voice called out. "Open up, brother, I am coming to look at your guest."

"Darn! Couldn't have found a better time," the old lady grumbled with discontent. "Now he'll start his spiel."

A short man with gray, curly hair entered. He wore a broad jacket over an embroidered linen shirt and suspenders; he offered a ritual bow and extended his hand to Abdziralovich.

"Ivan Karpavich Harshchok," he said. "Vasil's comrade, a metal worker."

"Warrant Officer Abdziralovich," he replied.

The old man felt at ease and spoke confidently and smoothly. He thanked the hostess for the tea and immediately asked the officer, eyeing the pin on his chest:

"And what political views do you indulge in, so to speak?"

"Well, for now. I'm still figuring it out; didn't get around to it at the front," Abdziralovich replied jokingly.

"Ignat Vosipavich is probably a close fit to the Socialist-Revolutionaries," Vasil noted matter-of-factly.

"He's had his share of trouble," the old lady interjected protectively. "Faced enough grief. Maybe he saw some goodness when he lived in the manor as a child. Went to school early, then quarreled with his father, and then the war came. Became pale from the sickness..."

"All this is nonsense," Karpavich loudly sipped his tea, interrupted her talking, and took out his tobacco pouch. "Do you mind, Aunt?" he turned to her and then politely offered some to the officer. "Don't refuse: what the soul has, it offers. It's good," he continued, saying to her. "A working man who has experienced sorrow will stand firmer. But one shouldn't delay with self-identification, so as not to be too late," he glanced at Vasil. "The young lad told me a bit about you. Told me about your father... It means you are for the common folk if you quarreled with him over our brother. Well, tell me honestly: if we had to stand up against the gentry, whose side would you be on?"

"Who else do you want to fight with? Ah, the old man has no better topic for conversation," Mother kept interrupting. "As if not enough Christian blood has been spilled. It used to be only: *Ah, if only we could have some land! Ah, just some land!* And now even when there is land, it is still not enough; you don't know what you want."

"Oh no, Auntie, that smacks of antiquity... No, we've kissed their hands enough," Karpavich became angry. "We must cut 'em to the root. Pity them? Like our Halszany Princes? The oldest hangs peasants in nooses, while the youngest runs around in committees, pretending to be for the common folk. No!"

Late at night, Abdziralovich returned to the hospital. Vasil escorted him to the main street. He shook his hand firmly and asked him not to take offense at Karpavich's words because Karpavich was a good man and did not think anything bad about him and knew that he, an officer, stood for the people.

IV

A bright face, sparkling black eyes, and unruly strands of hair; and in those eyes, a joyful, merry, quiet laugh — such was Alya Makaseeva, the eldest daughter of a landowner from N., who had made a great fortune during the war.

For the past two years, from the beginning of spring and until the last days of the season, the Makaseis lived in the Caucasian resorts. but due to the Revolution and famine in N., old man Makasei, despite spending most of his time in N., decided to buy a house in Pyatigorsk or Kislovodsk, and leave his family there for the entire winter.

The resort was deserted at the end of the season, and in the absence of her husband, Madam Makaseeva, out of boredom, willingly extended invitations to the officers who were being treated there[1], she saw nothing remarkable about these acquaintances and only tried to amuse herself and her capricious contrarian daughter, Alechka.

Occasionally, she would send a note to the hospital, prepare a table with fruit, wine, and cigarettes, and the youth would come to dance and have fun, drink and eat.

---

1. For instance, officers who were undergoing medical treatments at resorts and sanatoriums in the Caucasus region.

Alechka dreamed of becoming a ballerina, she danced often and with great pleasure, while her mother entertained herself on the balcony in conversations with Prince Halszansky, who did not like to associate with officers of simple origins because they had usually been brought up poorly. And the small black mole on his upper lip, reminiscent of a wart, could not soften his brusque aloofness, and sometimes even gave an appearance of silly, self-satisfied pomposity.

The prince made no secret of his dislike for Abdziralovich, the other regular guest of the Makasei house. And the latter felt the same way about the prince: he remembered that July night in the train compartment and the way the prince ate a piglet. And when in the prince's presence, the mother teased Alechka about Abdziralovich, saying that the girl talked about him while asleep and awake, and worshiped him as though he were a god, the guardsman remained silent as if bored, as it was already very risky to bring an unwanted element into his circle of acquaintances.

Alya had never, perhaps, loved before, and did not know if people generally loved the way she loved Abdziralovich.

At the park, in the mornings, he would wait until her delicate figure with curly, uncovered black hair appeared amid the bunch of younger brothers and sisters.

And he would be incredibly glad when they all rushed over to the bench where he sat; the boys saluted soldier-style, and the girls curtsied in greeting and then climbed on his shoulders.

She knew how much he yearned to sneak away alone with her into the depths of the park or climb a hill so they might enjoy themselves there.

They often reminisced about their first meeting at the Moscow train station, when she smiled at him and he averted his eyes.

They had already confessed their love for each other long ago and agreed to wait until spring. She hoped that her father would come soon; she very much wanted to share her joyous secret with the old man and boast about Ignalik. She did not trust anyone else. Ignalik would please Mikola Martynavich, she was sure of that.

One time, Abdziralovich started a conversation about her views on one's origins, wealth, as well as her stance on political issues, but she, it seemed, understood this to mean that her beloved was poorer than she, and she shut his mouth with kisses, asking him not to talk about politics anymore.

He felt offended and hurt, but consoled himself that it was the bourgeois way of life that was to blame, and she was innocent.

And now, having forgotten about that, he wondered, what was it that was splitting in his soul with such bitterness? Meanwhile, the prince, as if on purpose, set up horseback trips to the mountains or carriage rides to the Italian colony to eat honey and buy wine. And Abdziralovich had to invent all sorts of excuses to refuse because he did not have the money for such company.

All day long, he would be at the park with her brothers and sisters, and they would ask what was wrong that he was so upset; and with childlike simplicity, they consoled him, saying that Alya would return in the evening.

Sometimes he waited in vain until midnight and was torn apart by piercing doubt, wondering: does she love him if she seeks pleasure without him, leaves him alone, and is quick to believe that he has a headache whenever they are about to head out. Does she really love him?

One morning, someone delivered and hung a notice in the hospital that on that same day in Pyatigorsk, at the Lermontov Gallery, there would take place the first organizational meeting of Belarusian citizens, who had been thrown by fate into the Caucasian Mineral Waters region. The initiative group called the meeting.

Perplexed, Abdziralovich saw among the other signatures of soldiers and officers: Prince Halszansky.

So, he's also Belarusian, he thought, *how funny*.

But he himself was *nesvyadomy*[2] and, although he passionately loved his homeland, he was somewhat apprehensive toward the idea of a revival movement, of which he had once heard in passing.

When he arrived at the meeting, he discovered that the prince, who coldly nodded to him, was even leading the whole charade, standing on the stage amid the gathered lads and girls, soldiers, and several teachers-turned-refugees.

The Belarusians gathered with indolence and disarray.

---

2. *Nesvyadomy* (bel. несвядомы), *literally, "unaware" or "unconscious",* referring here to lack of national and patriotic awareness and Belarusian self-identity.

Eventually, many Ukrainians came, and then a large crowd of refugees from the Hrodna province arrived: elders and children, girls and women.

The prince delivered the first speech in Russian.

He solemnly said that he loved and that everyone should love the unfortunate Mother Belarus, forgotten and forsaken by us, because everyone was defining their identity now. He called for collaboration and unity, and to put aside mutual grievances between the gentry and the peasants.

It was impossible for Abdziralovich to understand which worm was gnawing at him the most. But in the end — nothing. Sickly soldiers and timid, but determined teachers also took turns to speak. Many heated words were uttered.

"We Belarusians have no class struggle!" the prince declared in a rich, resonant voice in his closing remarks. "There is none, there should not be any, and will not be!! We all, from lord to peasant, so to speak, will stand for one thing: a close union with Russia and the lawful granting of land to smallholding peasants!"

Thus spoke the prince, and no one among those present, sacrificing in the name of the homeland, dared to contradict him, even if they disagreed.

Abdziralovich felt his heart beating like a hammer.

Suddenly something seized him and carried him up to the stage.

In an enraged, angry voice, filled with fierce sincerity, he looked at the mass of destitute refugees and spoke in their native tongue, which he had not yet forgotten, and he sounded more and more terrifying as he spoke:

"The gentry murdered your fathers with their whips, and exchanged them for foreign bitches, and sold them like cattle... Your mothers were raped by young masters... They sucked the blood out of you. For a single birch twig from the lord's forest, you rotted in prisons..."

The prince-chairman slowly turned pale. The hall fell silent and thousands of sparkling eyes pierced the speaker.

"And now they tell you: you have no class struggle in the face of a common enemy... Oh, no! You do!" he shouted in a high, feverish, resonant tone, and he saw Alya's image emerging from the fog, heading to the mountains with her mother and the prince, leaving him. "It exists, this struggle, it must! Whoever does not recognize it, does not know the cold, the hunger, and you, you... Look at yourselves and remember what used to be! You are poor and despondent, your children are hungry and miserable, and you have erected thousands of crosses along the way, fleeing from your homeland..."

He sensed that his words were not what he intended to say, that the words were pouring out uncontrollably, but still, he carried on, and spoke for a long time. There was a thunder of applause, voices, a cry of an old woman — his speech was interrupted.

The soldiers abandoned the prince and gathered around him, as if choosing him as their leader. The prince, pale as paper, but silent and reserved, his pride intact, nervously drummed his fingers on the table.

The meeting buzzed loudly.

V

He did not see Alya the following day. She had gone with her mother to Mineralnye Vody station; they were expecting Mikola Martynavich to arrive.

At the park, Abdziralovich ran into the Makaseis' nanny with the children and spent some time with them.

Amid the talk about their father's arrival, the younger boy said:

"Our father really doesn't like "comrades." And the prince says they are hooligans."

"When you grow up and start to think for yourself, then you'll see, Valya, that it may not be entirely so."

"Why do you defend them? The prince said they'll take away the officers' salaries, and you're defending them."

The child fell silent. It looked like he was pondering a question but did not dare to ask.

"Do you like the commoners?"

"I do."

"I don't. They are all very stupid."

"That's not true, Valya."

"But the prince said it's true. He said that only those officers stand up for them, who themselves are from the commoners."

"So, Valya, you think I'm also from the commoners, yes? Is that what you wanted to ask me?"

The boy blushed and looked down.

"I don't know," he whispered

Mikola Martynavich did not come, and mother and Alya hosted a small soiree the following day.

An invitation was casually extended to Abdziralovich when they met, but he remained at the hospital after dinner. At the canteen, a military official sat down with him, a well-known Latvian actor-artist, who was suffering from tuberculosis and usually was not a very talkative man. He started asking about yesterday's meeting of Belarusians, invited the warrant officer to his room, treated him to watermelon and grapes, and touched upon his political views.

"You surely sympathize with the Bolsheviks?" he asked.

"No," Abdziralovich replied sincerely. "I do not believe in the possibility of an independent government of our proletariat or in the communist way of life in general. For now, it's a utopia."

The actor's cheeks flushed, and he suddenly changed his tone.

"Ah, I see," he carried on. "So I misunderstood you. I was told something quite different about your speech at the meeting. So, you're siding with the likes of our nobility, like His Highness, who, as far as I know, doesn't have much respect for your person and wouldn't hesitate to trip you up, even if only in personal matters."

The Latvian was irritated. Abdziralovich felt a sting.

"That's a different matter... But I consider the government's policy in its current form to be fair and I will, if necessary, defend it as a soldier must, against any enemy."

"Ah, I see..." he said again and smiled forcibly, deliberately. "Of course, against any enemy... It's better when there are no relatives or loved ones among that enemy. It looks as though you yourself, so to speak, judging by external signs, are of white bone."

To avoid a quarrel, Abdziralovich wanted to escape from the consumptive; fortunately, someone knocked.

"Come in!" the Latvian called out. The door opened, and a young Kazakh girl, a caretaker for the sick, handed the warrant officer a secret note.

"A messenger brought you this note," she said kindly.

"Ignalik! Come now. I am waiting. Alya," he read with joyful restraint in his heart and once more felt a kindness toward the irritated actor, and even a bit of guilt before him.

"Excuse me, please. I must apologize... I need to go," he said with a bright smile, shaking his hand.

"Yes, yes... it's alright. Don't waste any time: it seems you're in a hurry," the patient replied coldly and indifferently.

Abdziralovich hurried over to the Makaseis as though he had wings, but was late.

There were already many people there, including the prince.

He was sitting with the hostess near the samovar, quietly chatting with her about something.

Warrant Officer Kunst was playing the guitar. Alya and her two younger sisters twirled in a waltz with the officers.

By the time Abdziralovich approached the table, the prince had already retreated into a corner, appearing to be overly interested in some engraving.

The hostess of the soiree graciously extended her hand to Abdziralovich, but did not greet him with the usual jokes about his friendship with Alechka, nor with invitations to "help himself" at the table.

Once the dance had ended, Alya noticed him and quickly ran over. Her black eyes sparkled, saying that which only he and she understood. The girl playfully patted his hand, saying:

"Naughty, naughty! You can't be so late. Mother and I saw you in Pyatigorsk twice yesterday, and you did not have the courtesy to notice us even once. The first time, you were riding the tram. Then you were walking with some "comrades"... Mother was very surprised. It doesn't bother me, but it was a pity I could not approach..." and then she added, gazing deeply into his eyes. "Did you get my message?"

"Aha," he replied quietly, his voice trembling, and looked at the curly, shiny black hair, and realized with an unusual clarity just how dear this girl was to him and how much he loved her.

The prince left early; he noticed that.

Alya's mother seemed to retain her affection, yet, somehow, she was not the same as before.

Abdziralovich spent the evening happily, like never before. He danced with the girls, Alya's sisters, played something on the guitar for everyone with rare artistic enthusiasm; he stayed with Alechka on the balcony, and looked at the tiny bright stars out in the distant sky over the black silhouette of Mount Beshtau. He shared several events from his life, painting for her an image of his childhood and youth, and they discussed plans for the future.

She, delicate and frail, a bright face in the dark, listened to him lovingly, resting her hands on his shoulder.

At first, mother sent in one of the sisters with a shawl, and then to call them inside, so they wouldn't catch a cold.

VI

And so began the days of painful jealousy, despair, and mortal sorrow.

Alya seemed to have completely forgotten about him. She spent all her time on trips with her mother and the prince, going either to Kislovodsk, the mountains, or the Italian colony.

The prince had claimed his place beside Alya – that much was clear.

Even at the park, when the children wanted to play near the bench where Abdziralovich was sitting, the Makaseis' nanny guiltily led them away from him.

He was not invited to the next soiree after that night.

And the carefree warrant officers, who went there to feast and drink wine, lightheartedly said to him:

"Hey, give it up, Warrant Officer Abdziralovich! Is this really you? She's still a green girl, like the wind... And you know, too spoiled. How she shows off! Smokes, drinks wine, kisses the prince and whoever else in public. Even the prince is ashamed."

Abdziralovich wanted to kill them for such hurtful words about his ideal, but instead, he only forced a smile, waiting for the right moment to escape from everyone to be alone. And he only muttered in response:

"Well, no way. You just love to gossip about God knows what. It's not worth listening to."

They knew that he was suffering, were struck by it, but could offer no advice.

One early morning, when he, exhausted from a sleepless night, wandered aimlessly around the empty park and accidentally ended up at the train station just as the first morning train was departing, his eyes met those of the Makaseis' nanny by the ticket office; she was holding a basket.

The girl glanced away quickly and said:

"Alya is here... We're going to Beshtau station for pie, it's Valya's birthday today."

He did not respond but hurried to the carriage where Alya stood, waving a new, elegant cane.

Cheerfully, as if nothing had happened, she greeted Abdziralovich and began to tell him about their interesting trip the day before.

"Alya!" anxiously, breathlessly, and eager to tell her everything, he said in a trembling voice. "Tell me, Alya, what is this? Is everything really over?"

"You are trying to spoil my mood, although you haven't seen me for a few days. Listen, Ignalik, I cannot chase after you... What would everyone think! Am I to blame that you are some... some..." she paused. "Some kind of a loner and avoid traveling with us."

His heart sank, painfully.

"Why didn't you answer my letters?"

"Oh, here we go... You only blame me. I did not write because I hoped to see you. I hoped every day, and the days just flew by. Just think," she burst out with a joyful laugh, out of nowhere. "Just think: the prince is preparing to ask for my hand! Just waiting for Daddy. Oh, what a silly man, like all men. Although, you know, really, he is serious about it. What a suitor! Well, how should I answer him? He gifted me this walking cane. Look: with a silver mouse and such a lovely monogram!"

"*Be well*, Alya... right?" he asked in a sunken voice, despairing.

"Listen, Ignalik, if you don't want to end up quarreling, then leave the drama and resentment, do you hear me."

The locomotive puffed and blew white steam. The siren echoed clearly in the fresh mountain air.

They parted.

For a long time, Abdziralovich stood, looking toward where the train had fled, disappearing behind the forest trees and bushes.

She waved several times, wanting to cheer him up, but disappeared behind the doors sooner than he'd hoped.

"*Merciful Lord and Master! Please dismiss any thoughts about my daughter. And this my wish is quite natural, considering I am completely unaware of who you are and what you are in your social status beyond military service. I hope, as an Officer, you will fully comply. Makaseeva*," he read in a letter brought after breakfast, and collapsed wearily onto the sofa.

The prince dictated it! She knows all about his golden purse. He gritted his teeth. *And you, Alya, Alya! Oh, why, what was all this for?*

And a heaviness descended, overwhelming him.

Her bright face with sparkling black eyes and curly hair, girlish laughter, and jokes — it was pain and torment without escape.

His soul was torn into two. One half wept inconsolably, blaming the other for tormenting him with lies. And when he found some relief, it whispered: *Away, run away...*

VII

That quiet, melancholic season that he loved and that stood before his eyes when his thoughts floated to the huts of Belarus, had long passed by the time he arrived.

Long gone were the days when the weakening sun still scorched, and villagers lit the year's first fires under the ash trees. The smoke, gray and low, meandered above straw roofs, drifting upwards in barely visible colors. A thin thread of a spider's web stretched... A flock of sparrows noisily chirped from behind the fence at the hemp field, and a boy ran along the high and narrow, awkward boundary, among the green, thick hemp plants to drive them away, and they, with a whirr, flew onto the bundles of golden wheat in the field or into the forest. He eagerly threw gravel, thinking dejectedly that *oh, so much hemp's knocked down* and joyfully that *it's alright: tomorrow he would be taken to thresh rye and bring seed.*

Those days were gone.

They morphed into the day of a beautiful sunny morning, when the resort train ran from Mineralnye Vody to Pyatigorsk. It was too early in the morning. Sleep was oppressive. The passengers were dozing off. The sun was rising. The distant horizon was wrapped in a golden-blue mist, beginning to dissolve, while bright, joyful rays of light glimmered on the dogwood shrubs, telegraph wires, and fields. Where were the mountains? The area was already hilly; it descended in terraces into a wide, endless valley, then danced with rounded hilltops mixed with smooth, stubby strings of plowed lands, black as soot. From the left side, through the second window, a dark mass loomed closer from the fog. A sharp turn in the road, the locomotive grumbled to the right – and the mountains were close, so close... like on the palm of your hand, like in a picture or binoculars. A bare rock face, green clumps of brush. A mountain seemingly not so large stood alone, like a mere mound. But minutes passed, the train ran far, but it stood just as close, so close. Only twenty versts[1] left, maybe more. And the outline of the mountain forest that covered it was emerging through green spots of brush, grass and moss. This was the mountain-giant Beshtau.

That season passed like a dream. A bright, golden dream, and dark, heavy too.

He sits by the window. Alone. Mikola went to the other section of the building, where the classroom was.

Dark clouds rush quickly across the sky. They spread out, clinging to one another, gather into a single lump, and blanket the sky. An enormous dirty-gray cover of smog curled above the ground; it hid the sun. Tiny hands of the children, running with schoolbags over their shoulders along the deserted road lined with a row of sad birches on both sides, have turned red from cold. Snowflakes flow from the

---

1. Verst, a measure of distance. 1 verst = 1.0668km.

sky like white dust, pouring like orphans out of somewhere above. They emerge and softly settle on the ground, on the birch branches, on the pitiful clothing of the children, on their winter hats and shawls.

It's unbearable! So difficult. No newspaper for the third day in a row. Silly rumors circulated in the village. That they'd kill all the gentry in Russia. That manor houses would be torched.

Images surface in his mind...

The prince, pale as chalk, proclaims from the stage that there is no class struggle in Belarus. A large crowd of refugees – elders, children, women – suddenly rush at him in a mad frenzy.

Rostov-on-Don. The train station. The opposing Caucasus and Moscow-bound trains stand side by side for an hour or so. A restless crowd of people of all nations and classes fills the platform. A young dark-haired warrant officer with deep sadness in his beautiful brown eyes walks over to the first-class cabin, where both the new and the old public sit at tables: gentry and peasants in soldier's overcoats. Over there, at a separate table in the corner, there are two men: a dark, bald, intelligent Armenian and a reserved gentleman with curly black eyebrows and graying hair, with a sharp look in his eyes. Plotting something... Ah, but she said that is her father.

"Oh my soul, Mikola Martynavich, you radicals have had your fun! You want to go to the Caucasus, craving solitude?"

"I need to visit with my family," answers the other gloomily. He is silent for a long time. "We worked, we toiled, we created a lot out of nothing, I tell you," he continues the conversation as if answering his own thoughts. "And if there were more men like me, like us, if there were more of us, Russia would be glorious, wealthy, and powerful. But are we to blame for the scoundrels and slackers who come to claim what we've earned?"

Both men glance at him and continue whispering in subdued voices.

Doesn't Mikola Martynavich realize that sitting next to him is the one who loved Alya, his spoiled daughter? No, he won't help him now. His last hope passes him by. And the restless crowd of people on the platform suddenly rushes toward him and the bald Armenian in a mad frenzy.

And the soul is torn. Two souls. The one that cried and complained about the other for tormenting him with lies is becoming hardened, but also unkind, gaining spite and even cruelty. Let the other one weep for some maiden. This one does not care, and it will not flinch, even if the frenzied human mass tears to pieces the prince, and Makasei-the-Millionaire, and the smart Armenian. It does not care... But the other, the second soul, thinks and shudders.

Images surface in his mind...

Sometimes, amid the cold, grayness, desolation, and boredom of autumn nature, amid the dreary weather of late autumn, a little patch of blue sky unexpectedly clears up – one, then another, then a third. Soon, a significant part of the sky is freed from the clouds, blue, joyful; beautiful patches of color, dark on the inside and white on the outside, still float lightly along its edges. A black, heavy storm cloud still hangs very far over the forest, clinging on strong. But look, look quickly, how swiftly the remaining silver cloud has passed across the sun; the first bundle of golden straw gleams from the sky, carried by the wind, running across the bishop's orchard like a golden blanket – and everything becomes brighter, more beautiful. The branches on the old birch sway gently upon seeing the sun. And the frosty ground under the feet of a girl, who, having grabbed two buckets, runs for water, runs and laughs at something, wants to be softer, and even the sun forgets itself, lost in the moment, admiring the girl's beauty.

Sometimes it happens like this.

And then again – gray apathy.

A bright face with sparkling black eyes and unruly hair, and in those eyes, a joyful, gentle laugh – Alya stands surrounded by a radiant halo. And everything is happier and more beautiful. Alya! Alya!

Oh... once, he started a conversation about her views on family origins and wealth, as well as her stance on political issues, but she seemed to have understood it to mean that he was poorer than her, and she shut his mouth with kisses, asking him not to talk about politics anymore.

Or maybe she already thought that nothing would come of them anyway, so there was no point in talking about it in the first place, no need to reassure him.

Or maybe she thought even worse? Definitely! She thought he was after her wealth!

It happens like that sometimes.

And then – gray apathy.

"Yes, yes, yes! It happens!!" he rushed to the window.

"What are you shouting about here all alone?" Mikola entered, good old Mikola.

"I say: it happens sometimes... anything can happen! I just thought of an acquaintance. Mikola Martynavich, who shares your name, you see. I've never met him, but he stands before my eyes as though alive."

"Well, yes, it happens sometimes," Mikola didn't understand. "You know," he said, trying to sound very casual. "I got news from the children: Krupki was also destroyed by the commoners yesterday, Brother. The manor house burned down. It's alright, your father managed to escape to Mahileu. Our people went to the station and found out. So, you know. Nobody knows you here, don't worry. But your father, he managed to escape..."

Ah, yes, Krupki... Where I was born, where I grew up, where a portrait of a Polish beauty hung, and people would say: "Your mother died when you were born." The commoners killed her, as I discovered. Krupki, hayfields, my childhood... Well, to the devil with it, why would this matter? Is it not all the same? The forester's daughter Ira loved me but never confessed it. She did not believe that I, of noble blood, would take her — a tradesman's girl without a dowry. I love Alya, but I must give way to the prince. What foolishness! To the devil with it, with all of it!

"To the devil with it, to the devil with it," he muttered, alarming Mikola.

"What are you saying?"

"Ah? Father escaped? To the devil with it..."

"With what?" Mikola didn't understand Ignas at all and asked again. "With whom?"

"Yes, with everything. No regrets."

"The library, Brother, it burned down."

"So let it be. They will build one themselves if they need one."

"Who do you mean by 'they'?"

"People of the same bone with you and of the same flesh with you, Brother Mikola, but with a spirit not spoiled by civilization, like yours is, that's who I am talking about..."

"Well, and so what?"

"So what? Our grandfathers tormented yours, and now, you see, it's the descendants who are paying the price."

"Eh, Brother Ignat, I no longer have faith in the healing powers of the Caucasian mineral waters," his reserved friend joked, trying to steer his thoughts away from a bitter, foolish direction.

"Yes... they are poisoned."

Mikola paced around the room, at a loss for what to do.

"You see, Ignas, I have a favor to ask of you. Stay in the classroom while I run to the village. An old man is dying there. He sent for me. He wants to say something before he dies."

"Fine. As you please."

"I will find out the news as well. In Moscow, it seems soldiers are fighting with Junkers and Officers. Something, you know, incomprehensible. I won't believe it until I see the newspapers. It's been three days without them."

Mikola left.

The first-grade classroom was quite lavish.

Children sat quietly and looked at the foreign and silent newcomer stealthily but attentively.

Abdziralovich sat at the table, writing something. He lowered his head. He walked around the room. Once, then a second time.

The children got used to him and gradually became noisy again.

Behind the stove, in the corner where, on favorable days, you could get well warmed by the sun, sits a tiny boy with a frail, skinny body and a large head with hedgehog-like hair. At first, he glares with hostility at the unfamiliar man, but sees that the latter does not look at him at all. So the boy becomes engrossed in an amusing game. Under the desk, leaning a textbook against it and his knees, he arranges small cards with portraits of the gentry that people had brought from the manor house when they went to destroy it. He stands them up with various tricks and taunts, and, with utmost joy, gives them the finger.

Abdziralovich finally notices that the boy is trying to show off.

"What are you doing?"

"Nothing... just nothing, I swear to God..."

The cards fall to the ground. The boy lowers his eyes.

Abdziralovich picked them up, surprised: he saw himself as a little boy, the man whom people called his father, and several more distant acquaintances who occasionally visited his father.

"In eternal memory of a happy time, spent in the lovely, delightful Krupki at our beloved's..." he read on the back.

"Taukach is mocking the gentry," the children said in unison. "His father snatched a beautiful book with pictures of people when the manor house burned down."

Conflicting feelings erupted in him, coiling into a large, unpleasant lump.

One soul said: *This doesn't matter to me... It doesn't matter to me at all...*

And the other ached and was silent.

VIII

There are several small outposts located about halfway to the station. They nestle by the road at the bottom of a hill, living their own separate life that has nothing in common with those who travel in hired carriages from N. to the station or from the train to N. Those "in black" who smoke cigarettes at night, their yellow flames flickering, chatting, at times quietly, other times loudly, laughing and asking from the carriage: *What? Shall we give water to the horses?* And in the morning, they doze off, squinting their eyes in the chilly morning air, casting glances at the green-mossed and lichen-covered roofs of the outpost huts — and they move on, dozing off further, all the way to N. No one stops at the outpost to water their horses: the well is poor, the water reeks of rot, and a bucket is not easily found. Only peasant cart-drivers stop in the outpost, especially those from the "white" side, where people still wear white coats and white *magierka* caps[1]. "White" Belarusians also live there.

It's always quiet on the road near the outpost. Only sometimes in the summer, children with pale or yellowish, flaxseed-like hair play under the old, loaf-shaped birch. They

---

1. *Magierka* is a wool men's cap traditionally worn in Belarus.

wear long white shirts that reach down to their ankles, while a lazy dog with a shaggy tail and shaggy drooping ears lounges around.

The outpost field lies beyond the swamp, past the fir grove, on the other side of the settlement; it is not visible from the road. In the summer, the people work in the fields.

The outpost is even gloomier in the autumn. You can't see a living soul on the gray and dirty street from the road. Where are all their lads and gals, who should be enlivening the entire outpost? — only God knows.

A lifeless country. A silent people.

This was how the outpost had imprinted in Abdziralovich's memory, and he was greatly surprised when the sequence of his somber thoughts was disturbed by some movement on the road and in the outpost, and his solid melancholy was pierced by a resonant noise, breaking the silence of his memories.

Between the road and the outpost stood an old chapel on a steep hill near a narrow trail. The road was crumbling, red clay was sliding down, and the insufferable willows wouldn't help. Near the road and the chapel, a good peasant had put up a fence so that no one would ride over the grass.

The inhabitants stood by the chapel, sat on the fence, on willow stumps, and even on that hill by the road, dangling their feet over the red eroded clay, listening to an orator, but not all equally attentively: the opposition, or something, was abuzz.

The orator was a young lad, a student of the Agricultural School in Horki. When the wheels carrying Abdziralovich approached, the orator was standing on the fence, his one hand was grasping a pole, while the other, frozen, rough, and red as that clay, waved rhythmically to the tune of his hoarse, shivering, but young and strong voice:

"Brothers peasants! Brothers Belarusians! So, we will vote for our own list! For the Belarusian list! List number eight, remember!" and he kept waving his hand, as though blessing his listeners like a priest might.

The elders, men and women, listened to the lad politely and attentively, as did some of the youth, while a small group of lads intentionally heckled, trying to embarrass the orator. They were incited by a curly-haired old man in city clothes, who did not recognize Abdziralovich in his raincoat, and who himself only later realized that the man was Karpavich.

"Everyone must go to the ballot boxes and cast their ballots. Just take one day off, don't work, and go vote. Let not only the men go, but everyone: you, women, also," the student blessed the group of women with a wave of his hand (they did not even chuckle and continued listening intently). "And you, girls!" he nodded toward the girls' side.

The girls began to look around shyly, taking on an air of dignity.

This sparked a commotion, exacerbated by childish silliness in the chapel, unintentional jokes from the lads, and deliberately intrusive remarks by Karpavich and two or three others.

"Nonsense! It's time to stop!" shouted one of those two or three, some scruffy fellow, either a burnt-out outpost resident or a drunken stonemason from N. or the station; he shouted and looked back at Karpavich.

"Quiet, Kalistrat! I remember you from Horki!" the student-orator angrily gestured to the heckler and continued to speak.

But Karpavich pushed his way forward, eager to speak for the Bolsheviks.

Abdziralovich realized that these were the elections to the Constituent Assembly and wanted to stay until the end. His carriage driver gave the horse a nudge and threw him a bunch of hay.

The assembly was now paying more attention to the wheels.

The weather was misty, chilly, and dull. These times were much more suited for staying at home.

The elders, the weak, men and women alike, did just that: slowly and gradually, they were dispersing to their huts. Thus, the Belarusian side that supported the student weakened, and Karpavich climbed onto the podium and grasped the opposite pole. The student sensed danger and, straining his hoarse voice even more, he shouted:

"Brothers Belarusians! Brothers peasants! Men and women! And you, the younger ones! So, we will..."

"Comrades! Comrades peasants!" Karpavich's high-pitched voice rang out, interrupting him. "Listen to me if you want peace and land. Listen to me. I will tell you about the best program, so you can have both peace and the lords' land! Listen, Comrades, to the *Bolshevik* program, so you can have *as much of everything as possible...*"

And those who were wearing soldier's coats, and Kalistrat, along with a few others, even the girls, moved toward Karpavich.

The student did not stop in time, and continued to speak, though upset at the way Karpavich's voice resonated.

"Hey, youngster, will you give it up, or what?" Kalistrat grabbed him by the hem of his coat. "We won't give you our votes anyway."

"We listened to the youngster for a long time, and although he said he belonged to the Socialist-Revolutionaries," Karpavich pronounced the last two words carefully, syllable by syllable, "and even to some Belarusian re-vo-lu-tio-na-ries, as though our very own, but, did we hear from him regarding when we would get to divide up the lords' property? Why can't we divide it up now? Did we hear from him why we can't end this im-pe-ri-al-ist war right now? Did we hear from him about who exactly is running on the Belarusian list number eight? No, we didn't hear, did we? And there is surely only the gentry there who are looking to deceive the peasants."

"True, true!" shouted Kalistrat.

"But it's a Belarusian list, our own!" shouted the student and blessed his listeners rather crookedly.

"We don't need the lords' kin," Karpavich yelled fiercely.

"We don't need them! We don't need them!" echoed Kalistrat and the lads in soldier's coats.

Somewhat fearfully and shyly, the girls moved away from the student. The men started to get confused, too.

"We don't need your program, youngster, no!" shouted Kalistrat and pulled on him, trying to drag him down by the tail of his coat.

The student jumped off the fence onto the ground. He was awkward and clumsy, in big boots, and his open coat with yellow buttons and green trim flapped around his sides as he walked.

"Are you going to the station?" he asked the warrant officer. "Maybe you could give me a lift for a bit?"

"Very well. It'll be more fun together. Get in."

They rode off.

The assembly listened to Karpavich, and only a handful of girls silently watched their carriage as it left.

And again, a misty, chilly, dull boredom enveloped the deserted field.

"Why didn't you finish the fight?" asked Abdziralovich.

The student was silent, he grumbled and tapped his finger.

"It makes no difference," he said.

"Why?"

"Well... Let that Grandpa Bolshevik leave for Moscow, then before the vote, I can return here again if I or one of ours manages to get here in time. But now we need to campaign in S. district. Nothing will come of it here, because the question of peace and land is closer and more important to the peasant than the question of Belarusian revival. The old man is taking advantage of that."

"And are there many of you students who go around like this?"

"Quite a few..."

"Representing a party, or what?"

"No, of our own initiative."

Abdziralovich was becoming surprised and increasingly more interested.

"Where do you get such dedication?" he couldn't think of a more delicate question and was examining this simple, peasant-looking, and very typical Belarusian face.

"Where from?" the boy began more cheerfully, looking straight ahead. "Are you not a Belarusian, asking me this?"

"Belarusian," Abdziralovich replied calmly and simply, but with a hint of an amused giggle.

"If you're a Belarusian, then tell me: what are you doing to revive our unfortunate homeland?"

Abdziralovich smiled unwittingly but restrained himself and asked the student:

"You keep talking about a revival. What do you mean by that word?"

"You'd learn about it better from Belarusian literature than from me," the boy said coldly, already thinking he was facing an enemy. "But tell me, what are you doing for our Fatherland, for Mother Belarus?"

Abdziralovich laughed involuntarily and couldn't hold back, though he later realized he might have offended the boy. He chuckled and said:

"Fatherland – Mother Belarus? Ha-ha! Excuse me, young man, but my Fatherland is all of Russia."

"Ah! If so!" the boy suddenly jumped out of the carriage. "I am not going the same way with a renegade," he said without looking back, and continued on foot along a path by the road, under the birches.

"Young Master! What are you doing? Are you joking or what? Get in; we'll go faster!" Abdziralovich did not know what to say, as he did not understand the lad.

"What kind of a damned "young master" do you think I am?" the boy responded angrily without looking back. "I am a *muzhyk*[2] -Belarusian and I curse all the Russified gentry and renegades to hell... To all the devils! Do you hear?" he shouted angrily and veered off onto a narrow side path, walking further into the misty, chilly, and dull autumn distance.

"Stop!" Abdziralovich shouted to his coachman and seized the reins, intending to run after the lad: why and how did he dare to curse at him?

"Ride on!" he let go of the reins a moment later. "A fool, or something," he said either to himself or to the coachman, and added, calming down, "and he even curses too, what a fool!"

"A fool," agreed the quiet coachman and shifted the white *magierka* cap from his forehead to his wrinkly old nape.

And the lad walked on and on in his big boots.

---

2. *Muzhyk* (bel. мужык) a commoner, peasant.

IX

To live on and attain some peace, most people feel a pressing need for clarity and good comprehension of everything around them, as well as of their own recent lives. Such characters are most commonly found among Slavs and Eastern peoples. They demand fulfillment and peace of mind concerning everything that exists and happens in the world. From time to time, they simply need to organize their thoughts. That is, if not to ask the eternal question: "From where does everything come, and what is its essence?" then at least to soothe themselves, to ponder, wonder, and find clarity in the eternally ineffable. On the one hand, this looks like a necessary foundation for a person, but on the other hand – a superfluous and harmful thing at a time when "time is money."

The clearest minds are found among those of a very young or very old age. People of middle age do not have the time amid the demands and turmoil of life. Where and when to stop and think and ponder about oneself and the world, when everything around is spinning, as they say, in leaps, when everything around is rumbling, like a freight truck over cobblestones.

But even they sometimes find enlightenment unexpectedly on a desolate country road, after riding several dozen versts along it.

A quiet, deserted path through a wheat field, or amid the sad fogs of autumn, or even in winter, amid the white, frost-bound ground, provides the much-needed peace and births in the soul the necessary, albeit not joyous, peaceful clarity.

It also depends on the mode of travel.

The horse plodded slowly, clinking the bell on the bow. It sped up where the road was smooth and even, and also when going down a small hill; but it mostly just trotted: either down a steep hill, or over a dam, or again up a large hill; there was little evenness on the road.

When the unpleasant incident with the student-advocate was somewhat forgotten, when the sad and familiar fog of autumn began to envelop the heart again, Abdziralovich started to gain that clarity.

And like the silence of the blonde-haired coachman with a red, wrinkly neck, wearing a white coat and a white *magierka* cap; like the monotony of the road; like the numbness from the hardness of the sturdy wheels instead of the softness of a hay bed, which gradually lulls into a kind of slumber after one has ridden for twenty, maybe thirty versts without a rest; like the road itself – the sequence of his thoughts went on and on, and at the end of it, clarity was supposed to emerge, like a station at the end of the road. And there are thousands of stations beyond this one in the world, with many more to be passed in one's lifetime.

There was no clarity... There is that which he didn't know how to name but could imagine: a large muddy puddle, or a flood pool, or a ditch filled with rainwater, and in it a splinter drifts slowly, floating, then stopping, then slowly turning over there where it was...

There is no clarity because the most important thing is not there.

And where would that splinter drift now? Does he know?

The most important thing was missing. Alya? No, she was not the most important thing. What was, has burned out. Love for her has subsided, nestling in a corner. Or maybe it was never there at all, then or now. Even now, being near her might not change his mood, just as it hadn't at the train station in Moscow, when he noticed a bright face with black eyes and unruly hair in front of him, and calmly and easily averted his eyes, still so light and pure after his illness. And he still felt that joyfully cheerful, quiet laughter of the girl's sparkling eyes on himself. And he didn't look and was pleased that he had become new and different.

So, what was the main thing? The curly-haired old man, who offered him tobacco in a pipe, saying: — *Whatever the soul has, it offers,* — and who shouted, grasping the pole, interrupting the student: — *Comrades peasants! Listen to me! The best program...* — this old man knew the main thing: the struggle against the injustice of the gentry. But for Abdziralovich, this was not the main thing either; when one voice said: — *Join the party!* — another voice mocked its own other half and whispered with unkind smugness: — *There is no party for you! There is no party for you.*

—*But answer me: what do you do for the Fatherland, for Mother Belarus? - asked the club-footed orator-lad. — What do I do? What do I do? Wait! What was I thinking about, besides that? Ah: that the student speaks Belarusian all too well, and I – much worse; I lack words, especially for abstract concepts. But why do I need them, what would I need them for? My homeland is Russia...*

Drowsiness overtook him amid the sad autumn fog, the sturdy wheels providing a pleasant, numbing pressure against his side and legs. *I spoke Belarusian the most before the university. And thought in Belarusian, too. No: the school taught me to think in Russian. Is that really true?* And he was trying to catch himself while thinking: whether it was in Belarusian or Moscow-style, and he couldn't tell. *But you, however, answer me...* He can't answer anything. He can't even feel the full depth of sorrow and misfortune of this land, which is now covered with trenches, crosses, and graves. He cannot. *But you, however...*

However, he must do something. Yes, yes. *I will do it! I will do something!* The wheels rumbled down a small hill and dispersed the drowsiness amid the melancholy fog of autumn, which gradually lightened and grew more cheerful. Maybe even the sun would show, making one want to break away from the sturdy wheels and run down along the road.

X

van Karpyachonak Harshchok, or Karpavich (as everyone called him after he had gone out into the world), belonged to the old and long line of emigres originating from Belarusian villages, who still awaited their writer in literature.

This line found its beginning in the distant past when our forefathers, who were not chained to their pens by any culture, unlike their grandsons are now, suddenly abandoned their buckwheat farming and ran out into God's wide world to seek freedom or to soothe their atavistic inclinations.

This line also passed through those tearful times when our grandfathers, one after another, especially, as they say, the proudest ones, fled from their cruel lords, wandered around foreign, badly plowed lands, huddled in remote corners, meeting their end either in dark forests, or on deserted wintry roads atop white snowy beds, or on cobblestone by city fences, if they hadn't already been beaten to death for a crust of old bread.

It runs with old decrepit crosses and bones, and with burial mounds worn down by time, and during those quiet hours of mourning when a Belarusian in a white shirt conquered Central Asia for the Tsar, or headed to Siberia for all eternity for his faith, or freed the Balkan "brothers" from Turkish captivity, or laid railways across all of Eastern Europe, and wherever else, apart from, perhaps, his own homeland, and dug ore in the mountains and drained water from rotten swamps...

The line loses its orderly arrangement and sprawls in all directions only over the last few decades, as great many people were born, but the land did not grow larger; instead, it shrunk down to strips so narrow that even a chicken could jump across. People streamed out of the village in droves, to St. Petersburg and Moscow, Riga and Odessa, Tiflis and Warsaw, and far overseas to America, where there is a wondrous city of New York, with remote but wealthy farms owned by Germans and Russians, where one can earn a pretty penny, albeit with very, very hard work.

The line loses its orderly arrangement at this time because the lads from Belarusian villages started to leave not only "to go out into the world" but also "to make it among people." Schools opened, and one could become a clerk or a teacher, an official, or aim even higher: priests, monks, and even officers began to emerge from under the peasant roofs.

Each person found their own fortune. Mikola Martynyonak Makasei came on foot and barefoot to N., having worn out his bast shoes along the way, but the lad got lucky: he was now Mikola Martynavich and had many millions. Ivan Harshchok, or Karpavich, arrived in Moscow by train while wearing the boots that his father had left him before dying, but he did not have the same luck, although he had lived well among the monks.

A peasant's son quickly ruins his prospects if he does not soon forget his father's home. He then yearns for something unknown; in the city, he wanders aimlessly, but should he return home, he has no desire to work. And so he wastes his life for nothing: neither a candle for God, nor a poker for the devil, neither a lord, nor a peasant.

Ivan Harshchok was a fine lad, capable and skilled from a young age. As a young boy, he excelled in reading and writing. After finishing church school, his father set him up in a small school to teach grammar.

Harshchok, whenever he took something on, did so earnestly: he tormented the children with prayers, and the women and men — by reading them the "Soul-Saving Leaflet" with very frightening illustrations: a viper crawling out of a drunkard's mouth, a gossiper licking hot iron with her tongue, and so on.

On one occasion, Harshchok dreamed that he was a great saint or monk, and he heard a voice in his sleep telling him that he should go to a monastery to become a monk.

And he went. He joined the line.

He was a handsome youth: bright, agile eyes, curly hair, with a pleasant and cheerful demeanor.

Quickly and easily, he endeared himself to the Archimandrite; he was entrusted to stand by the holy relics when believers came, and to ensure that they gave money and that there was no disorder of any kind.

The monastery was famous. Many great lords visited there, especially after an important member of the royal family had been murdered not far from the monastery; princes and counts, princesses and countesses came to order memorial services.

And two princesses came.

They loved to touch the holy relics. And they would stand near the handsome novice.

And unwittingly, he slipped.

And then reached other kinds of disgrace. He stole money, defiled his body, and drowned his conscience in vodka.

Ivan Harshchok became lost.

He plunged into the most devilish abyss.

...Once, he woke up on a bare, dirt-stained, tattered bunk, slippery with cucumber and watermelon rinds and leftovers, greasy with filth, in a night shelter.

He lay between a shaggy, dark-haired tramp and a drunken, disheveled woman.

And he remembered nothing.

From the mouth of the disheveled woman with tangled braids, saliva dripped onto his bruised cheek. With one hand, the woman clutched Harshchok's jacket, and her other hand was thrown back — bare, missing a torn-off sleeve from her coat. Her veiny, dirty legs hung off the bunk, protruding from under her stained skirt.

Harshchok tried to comprehend everything, but he was nauseous, his head hurt, and he was disgusted by the appearance of the disheveled woman.

He craved a smoke, but had none. He freed the lapel of his jacket, and the woman stirred, smacking her lips, while the shaggy tramp ground his teeth in his sleep.

A fresh breeze blew through the broken window down below, from the murky outdoors, pleasantly refreshing.

All the bones ached when Harshchok moved to climb down.

He looked around. The night shelter was full. It was time for sleep. Thick, warm, stinking air hung, filled with snoring, whistling, and rustling.

In one corner, a dull murmur rose — some quarrel, hoarse laughter, and swearing — all in subdued, nightly voices.

He headed over there to get some tobacco.

It was the shelter's owners, its respected permanent residents, who had returned from night shift. Their spots, marked with a stone or a brick, instead of a pillow, were vacant, as everyone knew these were reserved, and that the owner would come and had the right to evict.

But in one spot, a tiny man lay curled up — naked, covered in black hair, either a gypsy, an Armenian, or a Jew — and the owner of the stone was furious at such disrespect for his rights. He spat in anger, then mercilessly grabbed the newcomer, still unfamiliar with the local rules, by the legs, dragged him off the bunk, and hurled him to the floor like a sack of fluff.

No one paid any attention.

The battered black-haired man stretched like a beaten dog and fell back asleep right on the floor, slippery and dirty.

Harshchok asked the thrower for tobacco. The latter swore, pondered for a moment, rummaged in his pocket, taking out a pinch of tobacco, then tore off a piece of newspaper from his greasy Moscow-made clothing, and handed it to Harshchok.

Harshchok thanked the tramp, went outside, and sat on a bench; he carefully rolled a cigarette and took a drag, pleasant and sweet.

His head lightened, his bones ached less, and he could now contemplate his situation.

The last pennies had been drunk away. There was nothing in his pocket. On him, he had a black jacket, patched up here and there with white thread, worn right over his naked body, ragged trousers with holes, and worn-out boots.

The silver cross, which somehow, even in his drunken and already *godless* state, Ivan did not dare to touch — because it was a memory of his childhood years, his father's home, and his *true*, pre-teaching and pre-monastic life — this cross was lost, either torn off or cut off by someone while he was drunk, and then pawned.

For the first time in all his revelry, the question arose: what to do now?

No one would hire a tramp to work, and he was a poor worker.

Begging? — a dreadful thought flashed through his mind. *Stealing?* — an even more terrifying and bitter idea.

After tidying himself up a little and pulling up his trousers, Harshchok wandered down the sleepy, mostly empty alleys toward the embankment.

There, street cleaners in white were already sweeping, brandishing huge brooms; women with baskets were rushing to the market, and various revelers were finding their way to the night shelter.

Somewhere far beyond the wall, a bell tolled and roared, awakening something sharp and painful in the soul. The autumn sun splashed across the sooty tops of factory chimneys, skipped over the roofs and domes, and raced, gleaming, along the rails; from under the tram park, a small, ringing bell called out, and the first tram ran across the river over the stone bridge, thundering and roaring, carrying one or two workers. Sleepy boats gently rocked on the splashing waters of the river, and flags fluttered above them. The distant bell tolled again.

Thus began the city's morning.

Carefully, as though sleepy, Harshchok descended a long staircase to the river, creaking his boots on the riverside gravel with childish joy, feeling close to nature that infuses with peace, and strength, and hope.

A fresh breeze cooled his hot face. Harshchok took off his cap, scooped up water in his hands, and washed himself, savoring it. The wind lifted his curly, long, uncombed hair.

He felt more cheerful now; the bitterness began to fade.

As usual, the city woke up merrily, bustling and resonating louder and louder, buzzing and ringing. Gradually turning golden, the red sun rose in the clear blue sky, bathing in light the glass of the upper floors' windows, roofs, signs, wires, and storefronts.

Elsewhere the bells rang, horses' hooves clattered over cobblestones, and trucks thundered with their long tar barrels.

Amid the noise, Harshchok walked quietly and out of sight, so as not to catch eyes with his shabby clothes, thinking about what to do now. Go home to his brother to recuperate? No, that wouldn't do. — *The vagabond came to overwinter on ready-made bread,* — people would say. — *Why didn't he come earlier when he had money? He forgot he even had a brother,* — they would say to his face and behind his back. — *But my brother is using my share of land,* — the other, his own voice, pushed back. — *But you yourself don't want to use it,* — they'd utter the bitter truth. — *You'd come home and start walking through the forest and oak groves to enjoy their beauty, but to dig up potatoes or harvest hemp.* — God help me, I don't want to...

He could not go home. And with what would he buy the ticket?

The only option left was to go to the Archimandrite and ask for a few rubles of what they had once "earned" together at the monastery.

He walked for a long time, following wherever his feet took him, and eventually, they led him to the walls of the monastery. Four years prior, he arrived here ennobled, full of faith and strength of will: he came to be closer to God. This time, he arrived angry and godless, hostile and almost contemptuous of these walls.

"Whatever will be, will be," he said aloud to himself and jumped over the cast-iron lattice gate.

The morning service was underway in the chapel. The Archimandrite would be coming out of the church. Everything here was so familiar to Harshchok. It was impossible to soothe the bitterness, the pain that scorched his heart, the thought that everything here had lost all its holiness, all its sanctity.

He'd already been spotted. Fat Paisiy, with a beard that was black like a spade and a shiny red bald spot, smirked under his thick mustache, glancing at Harshchok. He hid his hands behind his black belt for some reason, then took them out, and looked again at Harshchok from the kliros[1], continuing to hum through the church.

Thin like a twig, Nikadzim pierced Harshchok with his burning, deep eyes, full of undisguised anger.

Everything was sung as it should have been. Dark old women queued up to kiss the icons; they crossed themselves and waited for the Archimandrite to pass. Harshchok saw him, the way he, with an air of importance and holiness, blessed the old women and offered his red, hairy hands for them to kiss, all without even looking at them.

Moving with the crowd, Harshchok slowly retreated toward the door, where he was planning to approach once the people spilled out into the churchyard.

The novice boy, known to Harshchok, guiltily slipped by, rumpling his black curls, and began to extinguish the candles. It seemed he subtly nodded to Harshchok, as if saying: "I still love you even *the way you are now*."

Without waiting or asking for a blessing, Harshchok approached the Archimandrite and spoke to him, blocking his way.

The Archimandrite's neck turned red.

He understood what Harshchok wanted from him.

"An arrestee! Socialist! Go back to where you came from," the Archimandrite hissed suddenly.

Harshchok lost control.

"I'll go, I'll go," he was boiling over, waving his hands in great indignation. — I'll go, but you, you..." he switched from 'thou' to 'you'. "If you don't give me my three hundred rubles that I

---

1. Kliros is a section of an Eastern Orthodox church dedicated to the choir.

earned singing with you at the funerals, then you'll go even further than me! Remember the panagia![2] "

And for the unsuspecting old Archimandrite, these words came as an unusual insult. Oh, how much trouble and fear this secretly sold panagia had brought to him.

"Call the police!!" the Archimandrite turned to the novices, shaking with anger.

"Call, call them!" Harshchok shouted deliriously. "I'll shout about the panagia all over Russia, let them know how the clergy steal away the monastery's ancient wealth. If you don't give me my money, then I'll *do something else* with you!" he carelessly added the words from the letter he had written to the Archimandrite earlier.

An outburst like this looked all too wild in the church.

The novices pushed Harshchok out to the churchyard, where two constables were already running over.

"To the police with the hooligan!" the Archimandrite hissed and gobbled like a goose.

The mustachioed, red-faced constables were afraid of this candidate for the bishop and were well aware of the weight he carried among the gentry. They didn't argue or inquire, but grabbed Harshchok by the arms, jerked him, and dragged him through the cast-iron lattice gates out onto the noisy, glittering, ringing street.

"I'll walk by myself... I'll walk, I'm already walking," Harshchok protested to the policemen, pale from the hurt and shame inflicted on him. They remained silent and pulled him around the street corner.

---

2. Panagia is an icon worn on the chest of Orthodox archbishops.

There they hesitated.

"Don't feel like dealing with them," said the older one. "Well, you, Babrou, go to the post. I'll handle him on my own."

Babrou smiled, glancing at the miserable figure of the shabby vagrant, and walked away.

The older one, Simanovich, knew Harshchok from the time when he was in the Archimandrite's favor — at that time, still a treasurer and then, a clergyman; now he pitied him.

"Ah, Ivan," he said. "I know you well. You were fed, clothed, had honor and money. Why did you have to quarrel with them?"

Every vein in Harshchok trembled.

"And now, Ivan, leave them and find something else that suits you," the policeman reasoned. "Look where you've ended up."

He inspected Harshchok from head to toe.

"I asked him for something for the road. I asked him like a human being," Harshchok said.

Well then, Simanovich thought, *we won't go to the police and won't write a report, because for that the Archimandrite would have to make an appearance as well.*

"Maybe everything will blow over. But just so I don't get in trouble, promise me that you'll come see me tomorrow at this hour. I hope they won't ask about you, but just in case... you understand — duty, children... Well, go get some money, buy a ticket, and Godspeed back to your village."

Harshchok stared blankly.

"Right now, the cranes are in flight, women are laying out flax, picking hemp; they'll slaughter a rooster for the feast," Simanovich mumbled with a hint of longing in his gray eyes.

He took out his wallet and fumbled through it. "So, you'll come?"

"Yes. Thank you."

"Well then," the policeman hesitated. "I'm not harsh; here's something for the road."

And he handed Harshchok a bright half-ruble.

"Be on your way."

He began walking to his post, and shouted from the road:

"Be sure to show up, just in case!"

Harshchok, feeling almost defeated, rolled the coin in his dirty fingers, feeling a silent sorrow.

"Kru-oo, kru-oo," echoed in his ears like words; high in the sky, cranes flew over the meadow where women were laying out flax, and, to keep it clean, they raked away the golden-burgundy aspen leaves that had flown in from the faraway forest.

Amid the hustle and bustle, Harshchok headed to drink away his half-ruble, softening at the thought of returning home for life.

But anger still stabbed at him, painfully sharp from the helplessness and humiliation. *An arrestee, socialist... I'll show you what kind of an arrestee I am! I'll get you.*

The next day, when Harshchok came to Simanovich's post, the officer crossed himself discreetly.

"Praise God!" he said. "I thought you wouldn't come. Let's go to the police; they're asking for you, what can you do..."

He was led outside, where a dark carriage stood. They opened the door, shoved him in, seated a gendarme next to him, locked him in the dark, and took him somewhere.

Cushioned with rubber, the wheels of the carriage rolled softly over the smoothly paved streets, and only the horses' hooves clattered. Harshchok's thoughts raced: *What do they want to do? For what crime?*

He was brought to a guardhouse, led into a luxurious room and seated between two gendarmes.

Soon after, gendarme officers entered from another room. One held Harshchok's letter to the Archimandrite in his hands, the one that contained the words, "If you don't give me my money, *I'll do something else with you.*"

The questioning started up again, asking him who he was, where from, what he did for a living, why he intended *to kill* the Archimandrite, and whether he had any accomplices in the attack.

"Have you been in prison before?"

"Never, Sir Colonel."

The officer didn't like 'sir,' Harshchok noticed distinctly.

"Liar!"

"I am not lying, Your Excellency!"

"Right. We'll check."

They dragged out a huge album with photographs of various criminals and began to flip through it, searching.

This went on for a long time; it was hot and uncomfortable.

"Alright! First time with us, and there are no records from other municipalities about you," the colonel said.

"Anarchist, revolutionary, Bolshevik?" the colonel inquired further.

Harshchok's eyes widened.

The captain smiled.

"Judging by his writing and spelling, Sir Colonel," he flicked the letter.

Both laughed. Harshchok blushed — they were laughing at his ignorance.

"Well, you've described the monastic customs well here, but how dare you *threaten*? What do you mean by: '*I'll do something else with you?*'"

"That I would sue for my money," Harshchok replied.

"Ah, I see! Alright then."

They left to another room, and roared with laughter for a long time, re-reading Harshchok's letter, forwarded to the guardhouse by the Archimandrite.

They came back out.

"Well, do you want us to send you home?"

"I do, Your Excellency." Harshchok perked up, thinking they'd provide free travel for him as someone without means and not guilty of anything.

"Then write," they ordered the clerk and left. The clerk wrote a document, gave it to a soldier, and said:

"To M. transit-prison."

"What, through prison transit?!" Harshchok recoiled.

"That's right. You requested it yourself."

"That's not what I... I don't want to." Harshchok raised his voice.

"What's done is done. Take him."

The walk to the jailhouse, between two soldiers with bayonets and right in the middle of the cobblestone street, was long and agonizingly shameful.

Through prison transit, with soldiers... home... Oh, the shame, the shame, Harshchok despaired.

The torment continued as they received him in prison, wrote things down and questioned him all over again. An entire day passed — he hadn't eaten anything at all, not even a drop of water. He was finally shoved into a foul, dirty cell with bunks, overflowing with prisoners.

I'm so lost again, Harshchok thought.

Three months later, having been dragged through all the checkpoints and prisons, he was delivered to his native provincial town. During this time, Harshchok saw and heard a lot of new things.

He didn't stay at his brother's even for a month before going back out into the world again. He learned to work with metal and read all sorts of illegal literature with the same diligence with which he had once read "The Soul-Saving Leaflet." He gained respect for his intelligence from fellow workers and became known as Karpavich. But the intellectual leaders, with their characteristic, instinctual understanding, did not hold him in high regard. They sensed in Karpavich the kind of a self-taught person who might reach great heights in art, politics, or science but always retains some flaw in the fundamentals, and therefore, can unexpectedly and easily fall to the very bottom of human thought. Strangely, these people combine in their souls the best of humanism and the worst of nihilism, chemistry and alchemy, Marxism and palmistry, believing equally in both. Their gods love to incite strife and dethrone each other, wreaking havoc in the minds of their worshipers. These gods are usually too numerous, but there are also times when there are none, and such people begin performing all kinds of unexpected tricks.

I'll never confess to anyone, Karpavich sometimes thought to himself, *but I feel that I could be wholeheartedly in any party.* Indeed, at the beginning of the war, he almost became a true Russian patriot, then under the influence of his Belarusian student acquaintances, cooled off all too quickly. It's no wonder that he soon switched over to the Bolshevik camp. Karpavich sensed something familiar in Bolshevism, something kin and dear to him. *I searched for a long time and thank God, I found it,* the old man consoled himself and, feeling strength and courage, became decisive in everything. When speaking with others freely and smoothly, he, a short man, even seemed to grow taller from under his gray curly hair.

"We need to cut 'em at the root!" Karpavich said often, as he loved to, without losing his everyday sense of humor.

XI

Alechka knew that in her life streaks of good and bad days followed one another. She even noticed that her bad mood, that mark of the unfortunate, always started on Monday evenings.

It wasn't so much that Ignalik had left without saying goodbye that bothered Alechka, but rather that his departure marked the beginning of a bad streak. *They'll think I regret it*, she thought, determined to hide her foul mood from everyone.

"It was impossible to anticipate that Warrant Officer Abdziralovich would be so thoughtless: he left without telling anyone, almost as if he'd fled," she joked, forcing a laugh. "Even though he left at night, had I known, I would have gone to the station," she added, so everyone would understand that she didn't care about his behavior or his departure: she only talked about it for amusement.

The prince, however, understood her differently and raised his smooth, plump lip with a black mole, showing his white, frothy teeth without genuine laughter. He noticed that which she hid from everyone, and, at first with bitter patience, and later with patient anger, bared his teeth and did not want to, or perhaps could not, maintain a calm face before the suddenly detestable girl.

And for this, she detested him, too.

"Prince... You'd think he's so important!" she told her younger sister that day as they were getting ready for bed. "Everyone else is lower in status, inferior to him, and only he alone is good, one might think!"

"I never liked him," replied the quiet Lelya.

"And do you think I liked him?" asked Alechka and, not knowing what else to say, fell silent for a bit.

"Who knows with you," said her sister distantly and reluctantly, stretching her arms behind her head on the pillows. "You probably liked him, since you traded Warrant Officer Abdziralovich for him, even though he was so kind and fine."

Alya became even more indignant upon hearing these words.

"Ah! You, Lelka, don't understand anything," she replied quickly. "I couldn't just go chasing after that saint Abdziralovich when he didn't want to spend time with us..."

"What else is there to say?" Lelya directed the conversation to sincerity. "Mr. Ignat was not 'that one' to you, and you do him wrong by calling him a saint. Had you not listened to the prince discussing who's of what blood, you'd be better off."

"And what would have been?"

"That the prince has no right to talk to us about who's of what blood when we ourselves come from the commoners."

Alya blushed.

"You, Lelka, are so young, but you meddle in adult matters and understand nothing... No-thing-at-all, absolutely nothing! And it would be better if you never spoke about our family origins. Mother, you know, doesn't like that. Our mother is a general's granddaughter; only our father's grandfather was a commoner, and that was long ago. But you don't un-der-stand!"

"Maybe I don't understand, but you, Alya, do understand, yet you hurt Mr. Ignat... And now you regret it..."

"Lelya, be quiet! Fall in love first, and then you can talk... Sleep alone, if you're like that!" Alya ended the conversation in tears and left to sleep in the nanny's room.

At that moment, the bell rang in the corridor.

The nanny opened the door and quickly came running back to announce that Mikola Martynavich himself had arrived.

Alechka was her father's favorite daughter, his cherished child, and she received his love for her with pleasure.

Alechka was always very happy when he came and did not know what to do with her joy: she clung to his neck, smothered him with kisses, stroked his gray beard and hairy arms, and cuddled up to him, feeling that in the whole world, he alone understood her, forgave her mistakes and blunders, and loved her so much that he lived only for that. She was enchanted by her father's intelligence, his firmness in dealing with people, his wealth. She did not share the same affectionate bond with her mother, and loved her less than she loved him. For these reasons, waiting for her father was like an additional, hidden pleasure that saved her from great sorrow during the bad streaks in her life and added a special charm and sweet beauty to her happy days.

But now, when the nanny ran in and said that Mikola Martynavich himself had come, Alechka, instead of feeling joy, felt something new, strange, and ominous — either hurt or fear, or perhaps a foreboding of something bad. Her heart sank.

She stood at the doors of the nanny's room, looking down the corridor, where her father's large figure emerged from the darkness. She was thinking about something, and knew only one thing: she felt afraid before the new, the unknown...

"What, Alya, didn't you recognize your daddy?" Mikola Martynavich said affectionately, his heart overflowing with great love felt after a long separation; he delicately embraced her and kissed her.

"Daddy, I recog-ni-zed!" she replied and cuddled up to her father, but that new feeling did not leave her.

"Are you cold, Alysya?" the old man asked, noticing that she was not the way she usually was, as if shivering involuntarily.

And when his wife came in, he greeted her and immediately inquired about what was wrong with Alysya, if she was in good health.

"What could be wrong with her?" mother replied calmly, with a touch of irony. "She's healthy, just restless, ran around all day because she can't sit still in the house."

Alya heard what her mother had said and thought that she'd spoken without love. Hurt, she waited for her mother to start boasting about the prince, that he was certain to come asking for her hand.

A dislike for everything tightly enveloped the girl, pushing her toward the most unexpected actions — only Alya knew that this would pass, that this was just a bad streak in life, and for this reason, she restrained herself.

The heavy mood did not leave Alya the following morning either. She dreamed of Ignalik, as if she and he, and some other people were sailing in a boat on the sea. The boat overturned, and she clung to Ignalik, and both were drowning in the cold, frigid, salty, and muddy blue water.

From a white yacht that appeared out of nowhere, ropes and rubber belts were thrown. She grabbed one, but Ignalik, with a silent, agonizing, and forgiving smile, pushed himself away and began to drown alone.

She got up as usual and had breakfast with everyone, even though she had no appetite. But she did not go for a walk in the park, instead lying down on the sofa with a book. She couldn't bring herself to read. First, she felt a certain sluggishness in her body and a haze in her head, and then realized she was getting feverish.

When the prince came to present himself to Mikola Martynavich, and at the same time probe the ground for a proposal (since all the waiting was inconveniencing him and had become annoying), Alya was already lying under a blanket on the bed, with an old, cheerful man — the resort doctor — sitting beside her, and Mikola Martynavich further away.

The lady of the house brought in and announced the prince just as the doctor was stroking Alya's hand and gently reassuring the girl, addressing her so that her father could hear as well:

"It's nothing, nothing, my child: just a small disorder of the nerves... You need to calm down and drink my mixtures, although they are not very helpful, and this will pass quickly. Rest is the best medicine and advice."

Mikola Martynavich seemed to have no interest in examining the prince and carelessly gestured toward a chair for him to sit.

The prince was not pleased by this reception, and immediately felt animosity toward the millionaire. Alya only amplified it by turning away toward the wall when the prince had arrived.

After the visit, the prince understood that circumstances were such that there was no point in proposing. Having to deal with the "lout," as he cursed the millionaire in his thoughts, would be difficult. And the illness of his beloved daughter had steered the mood and thoughts of Mikola Martynavich in an unfavorable direction. It was in vain that the prince tried to start a conversation with him about different scenarios for saving property during the revolution. It was in vain that after lunch in the study, he told him about a letter from a certain person in Moscow, that they needed to — most definitely — save houses and capital and their own lives, as the commoners' revolt was no joke, and would consume said property, capital, and lives. It was in vain that he urged the old man to sell everything and leave the country; he listened absentmindedly and was silent, not even wanting to talk about it. He, who had come from a village, did not believe that a plebe would devour him.

And so the prince resolved to depart for the capital. That letter about the impending events frightened him, urging him to hurry.

He felt hurt. And he fell into despair.

In the evening of that same day, the cheerful, elderly resort doctor visited him, helping to dispel his sorrow and commiserate. They drank some Kakhetian wine, had a good meal, became red in the face, settled into soft armchairs, and smoked, thinking solemn thoughts. Then the prince picked up a guitar and tuned the strings to a minor key. The mournful sounds of the guitar drifted in the smoky blue dimness of the warm room toward the open balcony and melted into the gloomy air that rustled with yellow autumn leaves. Stars twinkled in the darkening sky, one, then another, and a third one above the black Caucasian mountain. The guitar vibrated wistfully, and the prince was silent, thinking about what had been and what had passed...

"Eh, it's passed, it's passed," said the doctor, shaking his head. "It was there before the war, but now it's all passed, all of it, eh-ah." He sighed, nodding his head.

XII

The cannonade did not subside for five days.

Machine guns and rifles popped and crackled nonstop, occasionally quieting down, only to flare up again with renewed ferocity. After short pauses, cannons boomed, drowning out the crackling with their deep, dull rumbling.

It was the fifth evening.

A gloomy autumn fog crept down from the gray sky onto the heavily wounded city, enveloping the cannonade.

Karpavich and Vasil were allowed to go home to get some rest before returning again to fight the bourgeoisie.

Dirty and disheveled, with machine-gun cartridge belts slung over their shoulders and around their waists, and with loaded rifles in their hands, they darted along the walls as they made their way to their district.

Occasionally, a concealed enemy would shoot from windows and hatches.

"They refuse to surrender, damn them," Karpavich grumbled about the White Guards.

"They say help is coming from Petrograd," Vasil cheered himself and the old man with hope.

"Oh, if only God wills it," sighed Karpavich wearily, internally chiding himself that he, a Bolshevik, should say things like "if only God wills it."

"If only God wills it, as they say," he added after a brief thought, having crossed a dangerous spot.

"Oh, we sure let them have it on Gazette Street," Vasil cheered up himself and the old man with memories. "A pity we didn't catch the party leader, that despicable prince."

"Halszansky? Indeed, a pity. His party is so-so: Cadets, Junkers... But he himself, he fights like a demon. He's everywhere," the old man said.

"He must have slipped into a vegetarian restaurant, or something, and hid there. I fired five shots at his back but missed: the prince was lucky to escape."

Suddenly, a grenade whizzed past them and exploded with a loud bang high up against a wall.

Lime and bricks scattered, and dust billowed up.

They quickly ran through the gates.

"Let's wait."

"As we should."

"Oh, I don't know how Mother is doing with all this," said Vasil.

"She's getting old. Would be a shame if she passed without saying goodbye. God only knows how much time she has left."

"*If only, she says I could see Ignalik one more time.*"

"Can't get that young master out of her mind."

"Well, of course: she raised him, an orphan."

"I wonder how he is right now. On whose side?" Karpavich said, curiously.

Suddenly, out of nowhere, there was a sharp whistle ahead.

"Stop!"

A crowd of people surged forward.

A group of local gentry men, scruffy and with raised arms, some ragged hooligans, and two or three men in military overcoats were moving up the street surrounded by armed Red Guards.

"Ours, ours!"

They presented their passwords and identified themselves.

"Ah! Comrade Harshchok! From Gazette Street? You really showed it to them when they were trying to flee."

"It just happened this way," Karpavich replied.

"Vasilyok!" Abdziralovich's subdued voice called out from among the group of captives.

"Ignat Vosipavich, how did they catch you?" Vasil recognized him in a coat with cut-off epaulets, and responded. "Comrade Chief," he asked the main convoy officer, "may I talk to him?

"I was going to the medical commission, unaware of what was happening, and no one detained me at the station. Here's a note stating that my weapon was confiscated. I was going to see you, Vasil; then I was arrested here. But I am a sick man and can't fight on either side. And I can barely stand on my own two feet, Comrades," said Abdziralovich.

"Do you know him?" the head of the convoy asked Vasil.

"I know him well."

"And I do, too," Karpavich chimed in.

"Well, then you may take him with you."

Abdziralovich happily stepped out of the dismal circle.

They walked on.

"Mother is very ill," noted Vasil.

"Oh no?!" Abdziralovich was worried.

"Yes, she's very ill. She will be glad that you came."

They had barely taken a few steps when revolver shots rang out from a nearby gate.

They spun to the side. But Karpavich, apparently caught on something, tripped and fell.

"Comrades!" he squealed in a shrill voice. "Comrades, save me!"

Several men from the White Guard rushed out of the gate, with Captain Hareszka, whom Abdziralovich knew from the hospital, in charge. They surrounded Abdziralovich.

Vasil fled and disappeared.

Tall Hareszka pointed his revolver at Karpavich, who lay helpless on the ground, looking small.

"Captain!! Stop! Have you gone mad!!" Abdziralovich yelled angrily, extending his hands in front of Hareszka.

He couldn't hold back in time and fired, swerving in front of the hands. The bullet only struck Karpavich in the leg.

"Ow-ow-ow-ow!" the old man yelped like a dog, clutching his leg.

"No need to pity such scum," the captain replied venomously. "Search him," he ordered, slightly kicking Karpavich in the side. "And you, Warrant Officer, how did you end up in such good company? Were they leading you under convoy?"

"Yes, Sir Captain. They didn't believe my papers and were taking me to their committee."

"Praise God for their stupidity. They could have sent you to meet your makers long ago. Well, arm yourself. I trust you will do as your conscience and duty dictate."

The street was completely dark.

The roar of battle quieted down for the night.

They stripped Karpavich of his cartridge belts and red armbands, laid him on a stretcher, and carried him to the hospital.

Like officers, they led and walked side by side. When Abdziralovich glanced at the captain, he instantly recalled the bygone days when his turn to go to the Caucasus seemed far off, and for a fleeting moment, a sharp ache stung his heart like a snake and frightened him. Physically, he had been feeling quite well by then. In the evenings, he would sometimes go out to listen to music or sit in the park square, mingling with people just to break the monotony of his thoughts. *The turbulent revolution rolls on past,* he'd thought then, but it was not just this that troubled him now. He feared that while sorting out papers at various offices, amid the infuriating sluggishness and uncertainty of the revolutionary times, his nerves might start acting up again, and then, perhaps, that which he loathed would appear – in the guise of a temptress. Another voice within him whispered that not everything was about loneliness, solitude, books, and thoughts; that one needed something else, something that could be shared with others, a cheerful amusement. And so, for three days, the warrant officer went through committees, unions, and offices until he finally obtained all the necessary documents, thereby somewhat quelling the snake-like sting. And on the last evening, walking along the crowded pavement to the boulevard with Hareszka, an old womanizer and cynic, an officer from a more peaceful time, he heard from him:

"You're only so holy-quiet because you haven't fully recovered from your illness..." Hareszka roared with laughter, adding:

"As for me, brother, I like to gaze into pretty eyes."

"I too enjoy seeing beauty," Abdziralovich replied. "If we relish the beauty captured in artfully carved stone or on canvas, why not admire the living beauty created by God?"

"Strange man! Really, a strange man!" Hareszka laughed, though he barely listened or perhaps did not at all hear what the warrant officer had said. "You're a strange man, you know, like a modern monk or... a cunning man, a pretender who finds love in self-deception, understand, my man? As for me, I am an old sinner; I like to look into pretty eyes; do you understand, Warrant Officer?"

Once more, Abdziralovich glanced at the graying hair by the captain's ear against the red, sunburned skin, and was surprised by his own memories and amazed by his sense of calm. He surprised himself for feeling no shame at not saying goodbye to Karpavich, and not even looking his way when he was carried off their path. As though he had no emotions.

The captain inquired about his life in the Caucasus and how the warrant officer ended up here.

"Our squad leader," he said, "also just arrived from the Caucasus and landed straight into this mess. He's a Guardsman, a prince – Halszansky, perhaps you've heard of him? A fighter, you know. Oh, he works hard! Doesn't take any

Reds prisoner, and those who surrender to him don't rejoice: they're taken straight to the wall!"

"I think I met him at the military headquarters in Pyatigorsk. But he wasn't planning to leave quite so soon."

"He said he was concerned the roads would be blocked; he has business at the headquarters here."

Abdziralovich spoke in a quiet, weakened voice. He couldn't fully grasp the frequent changes in his situation. The incident with the old Bolshevik, his injured wailing stood right before his eyes.

"Captain! I must leave you for a while to visit a family I know nearby. I will report back tomorrow morning," he requested.

Hareszka pondered and rubbed the thinning gray hair by his ear.

"Aye, you may go! But be mindful, dove, of walls and fences. What a joke it would be if you were to perish due to carelessness."

"Zip! Zip!" a bullet whistled past his ear.

People scattered in all directions and ducked.

"See?" the captain shouted after him. "And the devil only knows from where and from whom — friend or foe."

Abdziralovich saluted and hurried around the corner of the house, hoping to find Vasil or make it to the station.

Aye, *friend or foe*, he thought with a kind of shame or repentance. *I don't know who is a friend and who is a foe to me. I maintain bewildering neutrality and deceive both them and myself. Could it be that the noble blood running in my veins has some significance here? Nonsense, what foolish thoughts – that couldn't be the case.*

And one half of him, the one that understood the Whites, remained silent, numbed.

And the other half, the one that understood the Reds, demanded that he find the prince and kill him, and that he catch up with Hareszka and give him a kick in the chest, like he had done to Karpavich as he lay on the ground.

Instinctively and with disgust, he jerked the hand that Hareszka had squeezed.

XIII

She knew that death lingered close.

"Vasil, my dear... my darling," she whispered, struggling to enunciate. "They won't kill our young master, will they? Oh, Karpavich, Karpavich, poor soul, suffered so much..."

"Why would they kill an officer?"

"And he? Whose side is he on?"

"Well, I can't quite grasp him: it's as if he's with us, and as if he's not. Probably neither with us nor with the gentry."

"It cannot be that Ignalik would go against the people, not our Ignalik, he cannot... And our troublemaker, you say, got shot... Oh, Karpavich, old man, oh..."

The sick woman barely moved her dry lips, gazing with a pained and laborious stare from the deep sockets of her eyes, as her ghostly, waxen fingers nervously traced the edge of the blanket.

The lamp flickered dimly, casting a weary gloom over the basement. Vasya clinked and rattled with the samovar by the stove near the door. Occasionally, the distant roar of artillery and the faint rattling of machine guns would reach them — echoing as though a guard was turning a rusty ratchet. The red glow of a fire reflected in the window.

"Oh, my God, my God!" the sick woman lamented again. "I'll die without seeing him. And you, my dove, will you stay alive? Who knows? When will this storm end? Karpavich sprang and leapt, but only brought pain upon himself..."

"It will end tomorrow morning." Vasil replied calmly. "The assault is tomorrow morning."

"What assault is that?"

"We will all attack the Whites out of nowhere and beat them."

"Oh, my God, my God! How many more people will they kill? Give me some water. Oh, your poor mother, Vasil, will pass away soon. Our Karpavich, perhaps he's already *there*: we'll see each other soon."

Vasil remained silent and gloomy.

Thump! Thump! — someone knocked at the door.

The worker grabbed his rifle and ran over.

"Who's there?" he shouted.

"It's me... Ignat Vosipavich... Open up, Vasilka!"

Forgetting about the pain, the sick woman raised herself on her elbows, fixing her eyes on the door.

"It's him... it's him," she whispered. Abdziralovich entered.

"Alive, unharmed, my dear, my golden boy!" she reached out to him with unusual joy, and when he bent down to her, she kissed him, trembling, her frail arms wrapping around his head.

As he recounted how he managed to escape and reach them, and as they talked about poor Karpavich, her restlessness grew, her impatience barely concealed.

"Vasilka!" she called with humility and affection. "Would you go and find out if they went out to look for Karpavich?

The poor man might meet his end among strangers, oh, our heavenly Mother..."

Vasil left.

Suddenly, the sick woman began to tremble and called the warrant officer to come closer. Puzzled and feeling pity for her, he leaned over.

Glancing at the door, she trembled, wrapped her arms around his neck, pressed his ear to her teary, wrinkled face, and, shaking, whispered:

"You are mine! My own son... And Vasil — he's the master's son. I swapped you two when you were little, I switched you. I thought: you'd be happier that way... My own, Ignalik... No, you're Vasilka, and he's Ignalik... You are mine..."

And the dying mother pulled him tighter to her frail chest with growing fervor and intensity.

XIV

Several months had passed since her death.

Abdziralovich had such a character that anything unexpected in life did not immediately strike his soul with pain or joy.

In his youth, he witnessed a great fire just before harvest time in a large village near Krupki. The furious flames swept away yards and houses, granaries and barns. Children and women perished, all the livestock and the year's grain harvest were lost. Wealthy farmers turned into paupers. In grief, people tore out their hair, wrung their hands, wept bitterly, wailed, and groaned. Even old man Abdziralovich was moved. Having rushed to the catastrophe of his serfs, he threw himself into the fire and rescued people who were mad with fear. Meanwhile, Ignalik cautiously walked among the charred timbers and peasant rubble, a mere bystander, unable to feel the depth of the people's grief.

Similarly, since the beginning of the war, he had seen many corpses on the frontlines, sometimes even many in a single pile. Some of his peers lost their peace, sleep, and appetite at this sight, but for a long time, he remained just a passive observer and quiet thinker.

He had such a character that he did not feel anything deeply all at once. But as days, weeks, and months passed, as the tears of others dried up, he gradually became more and more affected by what had once been merely a photographic imprint in his memory. Deeper and deeper, he felt that which had overwhelmed others at first, but had since been forgotten by them.

More than a decade had passed since the fire when he happened to be in Mahileu on military matters. He loved this quiet, typical Belarusian place. He loved its quiet alleys amid sleepy gardens and small houses at eleven o'clock on a summer evening. He liked the Mahileu city clerk in a yellowish-white tunic with inconspicuous stains on the chest. Knowing that the official was eager to talk to the well-dressed traveler, he willingly chatted with him about the life of the small Mahileu gentry in the surrounding areas and nooks familiar to both of them (whence his new acquaintance, the official, had also come); and together, they criticized and praised the Jews of Mahileu.

He enjoyed sitting in a Mahileu pub, its doors open wide in the summer, under a green sign that read "Belarusian-American Bar." In the pub, a gray-eyed, round-faced woman with a white neck and soft, white hands, wearing a wide, simple percale dress served lukewarm beer and friendly conversation. She complained about the heat while fanning her rosy, sweaty, plump face with a small handkerchief. She asked if he was single, and if not, why he didn't wear a wedding band on his right hand. He liked to watch the hustle and bustle on Jewish Street, where he would be taken for an important merchant and duly recognized for his education, attire, and knowledge of European politics. In a pharmacy on the corner, they'd approach, asking: *Do you want to go to the city garden? Please, just straight down our street to the end and turn right...*

He loved sitting in the garden on a bench among acacia shrubs, on top of a hill, admiring the Dnieper, Lupalausky huts and orchards, and the valleys that glistened with gold at sunset. It was getting darker, colder. Promenaders chattered along the paths; orchestra music filled the air. Behind the fence at the end of the road, near the kiosks, local lads gathered and shouted in Yiddish and Belarusian, and among the chaos, a peasant man stood quietly, listening to the music and the noise, and silently marveled at everything and at the strolling gentry — so lonesome here in his white tunic with a hand-woven belt and a white *magierka.*

What was so strange about it? At that time, nothing seemed surprising: the local public strolled through the garden, while the peasant stood behind the fence and marveled at the "lords." A certain sadness enveloped Abdziralovich; he felt almost ashamed, tears welled up in his eyes, and he deeply felt all the great sorrow of those past, unfortunate, fire-ravaged days, and with it — the great, eternal sorrow of the Belarusian peasantry. It so happens to others that they cannot remember a melody or a voice on the first try. But, after days, weeks, months or even entire years have passed, suddenly, unexpectedly, with the smallest of triggers barely related to the bygone days, that melody would play out clearly in his mind, that voice would sing, awakening in his soul the image of a time lived, evoking a deep feeling.

Such was his character that the corpses seen during the war only began to disturb his peace after they had already mostly receded into the past, and their photographic imprint had sufficiently etched and left a mark on his brain.

Now, months after the old woman's death and the onset of the Bolshevik way of life, when the new had slowly lost its novelty, Abdziralovich, as if just coming to his senses, began to take in the old news...

He and Vasil buried the old woman when her body had already begun to stink, having lain on the table for several days until the streets quieted down after the turmoil. Only then was it possible to take her to the cemetery, ending the unnecessarily prolonged and grim task of the local burial. Neither Vasil nor he cried for her during those days or on the day of the funeral. They felt no sorrow in their souls that she had died, but they seemed ashamed of thinking and feeling this way, resisted expressing that thought and feeling, and maintained an honest outward silence. At first, the occupied table got in their way, and later – nothing. Only in the evening after the burial did they somewhat insincerely reminisce about the one who was no longer with them and would never be again. All the while, they were alike in their thoughts, remembering how she had always yearned to leave the brick cellar, longing for life under a straw roof, amid the free fields and forests of her native land.

"She yearned for it in vain," Vasil said, drumming a tin samovar pipe on the door, without looking at Abdziralovich.

"Indeed, in vain," Abdziralovich added from the table, where he was flipping through "Capital," and thought that her old bones would decay among the brick cellars of foreign Moscow.

Days followed one another. Vasil went to work, attended meetings, worked in the committee, and Abdziralovich rarely visited him, bored by procrastination and indecision. This continued until Karpavich limped back from the hospital. His wound was not severe and healed easily, but the bullet had stuck something that left Karpavich permanently lame. He regretted that they'd buried the old woman without him, but soon consoled himself for a good reason: the Central Committee of the Party offered him to go to N., to his homeland, and help the comrades in establishing the Bolshevik way of life there. This was the first time that Karpavich was entrusted with such a mission, and the old man was so delighted that he couldn't hide his proud joy for a long time. He persuaded Vasil to go, and did not object when Vasil, in turn, convinced the warrant officer to join them in N.

Abdziralovich liked the new place for its beautiful views. Wandering around the local outskirts offered a sweet relief from the disruptive Bolshevik nonsense in the civil service, where he had started working after being discharged by the N. military commission with a white ticket.[1]

He had a lot of free time. He boarded alone with a small, quiet Jewish family. He enjoyed walking and admiring the beautiful views around N., contemplating life.

In his memories, he revisited various periods of his life, especially his childhood years in Krupki, and was now

---

1. Meaning, unsuitable for military service, usually for medical reasons.

convinced that he had never felt that typical affection for old Lord Abdziralovich or the memory of the lady killed by peasants that children usually feel for their parents. It seemed to him that he had always had more affection and sense of kinship for the deceased mother than for them, although without knowing that she was not just his beloved *Nanny Malanka*, but his own mother. And now he thought: *Well, I know my mother's secret, but what has changed in my thoughts or feelings? Nothing...*

Yet an impartial observer, looking at him from the outside and considering every movement of his inner life, would say that although the dying mother's confession did not alter his stance toward the people who were close to him — mother, old Abdziralovich, the slain lady, Vasil — in one way or another, but unbeknownst to him, this confession had changed his attitude or, rather, his views on the social revolution and on his own participation in the establishment of the new way of life. Previously, he was as if on the outside, away from the people, the peasant and worker community, observing the revolutionary turmoil the way he'd once observed the great fire in the village – that is, as only an outsider can. Previously, when he saw how at every station, at every verst — and the closer to the front lines, the more catastrophically — crumbled the life of the great empire, created by the bloody blisters and sweat of that community, when he saw how, along with it, perished the last shred of honesty and the last hope that it might still cling to a twig and not be shattered into tiny fragments under the mountain; previously, when thinking about everything that was happening around him, he placed himself on the outside, away from the people's misfortune, beyond the accursed line, only occasionally throwing up his hands, like a well-meaning stranger over someone else's misfortune. Now, having heard his mother's confession, he suddenly felt himself a part of the community, outside of which he had stood before. When previously, he looked at the attempts of various unscrupulous enthusiasts to control the unfortunate human herd as though they were madmen who temporarily reigned with impunity, now, he painfully noted every injustice on their part, all the while remaining true to his character, just a passive observer and a quiet thinker. At the same time, he increasingly disliked those officers who kept leaving the Bolshevik realm, and progressively resented the saboteurs within that realm. Nevertheless, he was also pleased that he himself had been discharged from the army with a white ticket.[2]

---

2. A fragment of the manuscript of *Two Souls*, beginning with this line, had not been returned by the representatives of the occupying authorities, who conducted a search in July 1919 in the offices of 'Belarusian Thought', where the story was published.

XV

Evening hour. The sun had set, leaving only a red streak on the western horizon above the quiet grove.

The tranquil field, the peaceful huts, the whispering orchard, and the birch tree near the well – everything was ready to sleep.

Occasionally, a branch or a leaf on the pear tree would stir, as if wanting to play with the slight breeze, but then, forsaken by it, it would fall still again, ready for the night's prayer and silence.

Who knew where that breeze had disappeared off to, but the summer sky breathed with languid stillness, dark and sultry.

The festive day was over. The noise from the outpost streets had died down. A group of men and women, who had been sitting and chatting on the logs and stumps collected during the previous autumn from the master's forest, gradually dispersed in all directions. Everything was under the rule of the August night, spreading its intoxicating, heavy spell, as though reluctantly finding its way into every corner.

The earth slept...

But Mikola Kantsavy couldn't sleep. He stepped out of the house, petted Zhuk, walked through the orchard, and entered the haze of a humid field, right on the border, amidst the tall and fragrant hemp. Far beyond the forest, in the sky, the distant stars flickered and dimmed.

Late evening... The wheat and the dusty road had quieted down in the dark. Late evening.

Sounds still carried from the pasture beyond the village, from the furthest huts. Horses neighed and stamped their feet, unseen.

The night watchmen were setting out.

Gates creaked open, a hinge rasped, a dog barked, a bucket squeaked near the well, and then, one after another, the watchmen rode out, disappearing into the dark road toward the fields.

"Hey, hey! Fiu-fsi-si! Kos, kos!"

Young lads on horseback kicked them in the sides, but the horses, unyielding, moved slowly, gently shifting their limbs.

At first, the lads were restless. Taukach whistled. Blyshka played a quadrille, and Kastyuchok, a student from the second division who climbed trees like a cat, sang a song:

> "My handkerchief is
> blowing in the wind,
> My beloved fights in the
> war..."

But the enchantment of that sultry night quieted them. They fell silent.

There was a long silence everywhere. It seemed they heard a noise. No, it was a bird crying out. No, not a bird – far in the distance, someone was talking or singing along the road.

The teacher walked toward the sounds, which grew louder and closer.

Ripe wheat lined the road to N.

Among the wheat, behind a hill, two voices chattered. Mikola recognized them as Ira and Sukhavey, a clumsy student from Horki. They were probably coming to him. Good. He was glad. But what news would they bring about the sacred cause of the Motherland's revival? What were they discussing?

"I prefer Yakub Kolas," Sukhavey said with comical seriousness, "because in his verses, I hear what I feel here and now, under Belarusian sky, amid Belarusian wheat, that truly Belarusian spirit that is the hallmark of Belarusian poetry and no other..."

"And I like Yanka Kupala because in his work you can find that spirit too, but also better poetical technique than Kolas," Ira responded to him with affection.

"And I like both of them," Mikola happily stepped out onto the road from the darkness, greeting them. He thought: *only conversations about Belarus everywhere, always.*

They were a bit startled by the surprise but joyfully greeted him.

"We're coming to you, Mikola Navumavich, apologies for being delayed," Ira said with her soft, slightly trembling, rich inner voice. "To you, and with an important matter...

What kind of important matter? the teacher wondered impatiently, but he endured, not wanting to ask until they reach his house.

"It's very important, but it's not appropriate to discuss in the field," Sukhavey noted formally.

"Well, of course!" Ira shouted playfully. "We can't discuss serious matters in the fields when there is such poetry around! Oh, what a wonderful, magical night!"

She extended her arms in the darkness that was filled with the aroma of ripe wheat: "But, dear friends! My poor legs will accept all this poetry if we sit for an hour, just a little bit, amid the scent of this sultry night and ripe wheat... Oh, let us sit!"

"You know, there is a nice clearing right to the side from here, under a pear tree," suggested Mikola, leading the lad and the girl with him.

They all sat down under the drowsy pear tree and remained silent, barely able to see one another in the dark. Ira began to recite:

"Good night, dawn and
twilight!
The mist already lies upon
the earth,
Covering all with a black
robe,
Illuminating the sky with
dusty stars.
Silence envelops my
soul!
The breeze barely stirs

the roadside pear,

Gently swaying,

whispering,

The fireflies laugh

sweetly in the silence,

The spring softly tinkles

in the distance.

Good night, dawn and

twilight!"

Mikola and Sukhavey felt somewhat embarrassed by this unexpected joy. They wanted to say something, so as not to be silent, but could find no words. They remained silent, the girl was silent, and the night was silent.

"Guess whose poem that is?" Ira asked, trying to break the silence.

"The *late* Maksim Bahdanovich!" they replied in unison, and a sense of melancholy enveloped all three. Silence. The wound was fresh; it still ached. Ira continued to recite... "'On the Occasion of the Death of Maksim Bahdanovich' — a poem by Yasakar," she announced to the night, to the wheat, to the pear tree, and to the entire field. And the more she recited, the more inspired she became, and her trembling, emotion-filled voice stirred every living and non-living thing around her:

"Spring lyre, enchanting

lyre,

Played in the morning

about the sun;
And strings sang of the
starry expanse,
And strings sang
endlessly;
Their sounds enticed
earthly expanses,
And songs poured in
waves,
And echoes awakened
secret dreams,
And people wept in
sorrow..."

Mikola felt tears drop from his eyes, and silently berated himself for being so emotional, then defended himself that it was good that he cried for the bard who'd perished so soon, and was glad that his companions couldn't see his tears in the dark. Ira carried on:

"One cannot help but
weep, when hearing a
loved one in the distant
land
Speak of the savior of the
poor;
One cannot help but
weep for the native land,
Where mockery,

suffering, and grief
prevail.
The poet's soul knew no
peace,
For his thoughts raced
toward the heights;
They raced to the forests,
to the river's flow.
He played, but the strings
kept breaking...
Breaking, for his powerful
cries
Were too strong, too
overwhelming...
With the lyre's strings,
the soul's strings
Broke...
...Far from the native
border
Our poet took the eternal
road,
That leads all the way to
God.
For the flame of the heart
burned – but it did not
warm,
In that flame, the heart
burned out..."

Without finishing the poem, the usually cheerful girl fell silent, sitting somberly with them for a long time.

"Where did you get this poem, Iraida Auhenauna?" the teacher asked.

"Let our friend Sukhavey speak, as I'm tired," she replied. "I want to be silent and listen."

"To tell you, Uncle, about where this poem is from would mean to open a discussion about all kinds of things," the young man began, "but I think no one is eavesdropping here, so we can speak freely. So, you see, one of our students came from Minsk, from beyond the demarcation line, and delivered some literature."

The lad briefly summarized all the news.

"But the main thing is this," he added at the end, "the student brought a letter from Vilnia addressed to you. It's from a very wealthy Mr. Abdziralovich to be forwarded to his son, some former Warrant Officer Abdziralovich. The letter is with me, in my pocket; I'll give it to you when we get to your place, as it's too dark here anyway. When the student mentioned the letter in Horki, at a general meeting while reporting on the current Belarusian life beyond the demarcation line, Iraida Auhenauna was there. We all know what old Abdziralovich is writing about to his son. He feels his death approaching and wants to reconcile with his son, and, at the same time, leave all his wealth to him. Having learned about this, Iraida Auhenauna made a statement that she had once been acquainted with the Abdziralovichs and she did not believe that the Warrant Officer Abdziralovich would respond to his father's invitation. The money, and it is Belarusian money earned by Belarusian toil and on

Belarusian land, could be lost if young Abdziralovich cannot be persuaded to take it, even at the price of reconciliation with his unloved, hated father. He must take the money!.. If not for himself, then for the cause of the Motherland's revival... Do you understand? In any case, these funds, or at least a portion of them, must pass through the hands of Warrant Officer Abdziralovich and yours, Uncle, for the cause..."

The student struggled to express his thoughts as clearly as he wished. He fell silent, hoping that the girl would help him explain everything to the teacher, as she was well informed about these matters and had proposed the idea to begin with. But she stubbornly remained silent. And so did Kantsavy, overwhelmed by unexpected and joyful thoughts that enveloped him. The lad continued:

"So, Uncle, we came to you on behalf of all our friends to discuss this important matter more thoroughly, because we hoped you would know best what to do. We asked Iraida Auhenauna to accompany you to young Abdziralovich, as his old acquaintance, for negotiations, but for some reason, she refuses. She only agreed to come to you."

"For the Belarusian cause, I'll do anything, but I asked and continue to ask not to pressure me to negotiate with Abdziralovich..." the girl said a little nervously. "I think there is no reason for me to go... Mikola Navumavich can handle it alone just fine. And if that's the case, why don't you, dear Sukhavey, go with Mikola Navumavich?"

Sukhavey didn't like long conversations where everything seemed obvious and clearly needed for the cause. But here, he had to gather all his patience and tact.

"So you see, my friend," he started to explain to her in a formal tone, with a slightly ironic tone, "you shouldn't just go as his former acquaintance, familiar with all the details about the situation, but more than anything, you should go as a woman. You can persuade Abdziralovich better than I can, better than any man, and maybe even better than Uncle Kantsavy, with all the required tact and care... If he still harbors resentment against his father for being a landowner, and a bad one at that, you, with your delicate feminine nature, are best suited to persuade him, perhaps, a completely *nesviadomy* Belarusian or a renegade, to take his father's money for the Belarusian cause. But if his mood is nowhere close to this, then he might find our intrusion into his personal affairs bewildering, and he might be glad to inherit his father's wealth, and here again, you are best suited to stand down at the right moment and only extend a request that he gives a little bit toward, for example, our theater club, in return for our help in his negotiations with his father and for having inconvenienced us to begin with."

"I cannot and will not go," the girl replied firmly.

Kantsavy only listened, thinking to himself.

The night deepened, losing its drowsy languor. The distant stars flickered sparsely, while the leaves on the sleepy pear tree rustled more frequently. It was time to go inside.

XVI

Mikola Kantsavy, a teacher and an honorable friend of Abdziralovich, had hosted him during his journey from the Caucasus to Moscow. He had often regretted that Ignas, who seemed capable and educated, was lost to the holy cause of the revival, perishing as a renegade.

Amid the endless and all-consuming daily grind, Mikola would forget about him; only when the shortage of *sviadomy* workers among the Belarusian intelligentsia became painfully evident did he remember his friend, scolding himself for not having guided Ignas toward the Belarusian idea sooner.

He both blamed and exonerated himself for that oversight, recalling the shame that had overtaken him when he first attempted to *advocate* to Ignas.

Mikola hadn't fully understood the reasons for his shame but thought that it stemmed from his deep affection for Ignas, who was then grappling with introspection, and from his profound respect for Ignas's thoughts and convictions. Mikola had always considered Ignas intellectually and generally more developed than himself.

Mikola sensed that Ignas would eventually see the truth and come to it on his own, perhaps even leading others like him. He thought that trying to persuade Ignas would be unnatural. Besides, it would be shameful to try explaining to Ignas something that one should only have to explain to an ignorant, illiterate person who does not even realize he is a Belarusian. Moreover, Mikola and Ignas had come out from the same school, where both of them were simply considered "Russians," with no awareness of Belarusian identity. This added to Mikola's reluctance to persuade Abdziralovich, as if he could teach a grown, capable man a new alphabet instead of the false one that the Moscow school had given them.

Ignas Abdziralovich and the alphabet, even a new one – truly, it is a disgrace if a man like him requires one, Mikola thought about his dear friend, but did not judge him, knowing there must be significant, justifiable reasons for this, though this aspect, due to lack of time, remained the least clear for the teacher. Besides, Mikola Kantsavy felt that, given the war and revolution, the revival movement had achieved colossal success, making much of the advocacy needed five years ago no longer necessary... He believed that all renegade Belarusians knew about the revival and their duty to partake in it, and if they didn't, then it was due to sheer negligence or corrupt nature. Of course, in Mikola's eyes, Abdziralovich belonged to the category of the negligent, and not the corrupt renegades. And even the negligence of Abdziralovich could have blameless reasons; that's how much Mikola loved and respected him.

Lately, Mikola Kantsavy found himself in a lively, elevated mood, shedding his former timidity, quietness, and agreeableness in front of others. The Belarusian cause was spreading like a great wave through the surrounding sea of peasantry, seemingly expanding the teacher's spirit and inner being... The movement was increasingly taking on a social character. The harmony of the earlier, predominantly national peculiarities of the movement with the current social peculiarities filled Mikola's heart with unusual joy, for he was fully convinced that only on the social and national path would the Belarusian revival be certain and capable of swiftly encompassing the vast masses of Belarusian peasantry.

And not only the peasantry but also the Belarusian bourgeoisie, wherever it still existed and retained much of its Belarusian character and ideals. Mikola saw this bourgeoisie in some provincial and district towns in Eastern Belarus, which he visited on occasion, and he never forgot in his remote village corner that this very bourgeoisie could still play a crucial role in combating the lingering, damned Russifying influence across contemporary Belarusian cities, largely *Belarusian* in name only. The social aspect of the revival would capture the most worthwhile, valuable and cultured parts of the remaining Belarusian bourgeoisie!

Students from Horki, who added a certain system and organization to the work and with whom Mikola and other teachers had a well-established connection and constant communication, gave him further hope through their conversations and reports about their advocacy and educational activities throughout the entire homeland, especially in the Horki area and the eastern half of Belarus, where the work was not hindered by differences of faith with the Muscovites like it was in the West, and where the social foundation was much better prepared. These results of

Belarusian work, which improved among the peasantry with their growing reaction against the Bolshevik way of life, also gave him hope.

As a sincere and gentle man, Mikola acknowledged that his happiness at this reaction was not entirely blameless and commendable, as it could place him alongside the hated enemies of the people and justice, and so there was not much to rejoice about, as the idea of a *national Bolshevism*, a term he had inadvertently coined in his mind, had never dimmed in peasant consciousness; it was the contemporary form of the Bolshevik idea that repelled them due to external reasons like the blockade of Bolshevik territory, and internal reasons like the commissars' crimes and incompetence. For his own peace of mind, Mikola noted that there would not be any joy for him at all, had the overwhelming majority of Bolsheviks known to him not been (unbeknownst to themselves) a Muscovite force or simply a force hostile to the Belarusian revival.

Mikola, like all revivalists, had difficulty accepting that, in addition to foreigners, it was the worst of the Belarusian people, or *muscovitized*[1] Belarusians, who ended up in Bolshevism and now ruled over the Belarusian peasantry, along with incorrigible renegades and stupid party oppositionists of "any kind of revival," who, in their wretched fanaticism, held in contempt the Belarusian language and everything Belarusian. So, Mikola knew the price of his joy due to the peasants' dislike of the Bolsheviks,

---

1. *Muscovitized*, meaning russified.

yet he rejoiced, seeing the mood of the peasants as beneficial to the movement.

If the same mood prevails among the peasants beyond the demarcation line, thought the teacher, *the leaders of the Belarusian movement will surely manage to create a Belarusian army by the time the Germans exit Belarus and they will defend the homeland with armed force! And then... and then...* his thoughts raced faster and faster, losing order and cohesion with their detachment from reality.

Elated, Mikola now often experienced a kind of nervous excitation that easily clouded his mind and burned his cheeks. But it was not only due to the happiness at Belarusianism taking root but also because he had become involved in a dangerous fight that carried a threat of severe "extraordinary" measures. When images of arrest and interrogations in the "extraordinary commission"[2] or tribunal floated before his eyes — in his thoughts, he involuntarily sought out those who would stand up for him before the Bolshevik dictators, and he felt pleasantly elated, intoxicated, and moved by these thoughts. Then his mind turned to Abdziralovich. On one occasion, Abdziralovich wrote to Mikola, saying he lived in N., and had once saved the life of a Bolshevik factory supervisor in N., the limping Harshchok, implying proximity to the Bolshevik elite. So

---

2. *bel.* «чразвычайка», lit. "extraordinary commission" or Cheka. Cheka was the first in a succession of Soviet secret police organizations, set up to protect the revolution from reactionary forces, i.e. "class enemies", bourgeoisie, clergy, and all political opponents of the communist regime. Cheka performed mass arrests, imprisonments, torture, and executions without trial. Cheka was the predecessor of NKVD.

he could have him freed even from the "extraordinary commission." And so he frees his Mikola... So daydreamed the teacher, suddenly blushing at the thought of indulging in such childishness during the time of a harsh, bloody struggle. And, thinking about his friend, he again regretted not turning Abdziralovich into a vigorous worker for the Belarusian revival.

XVII

***

After graduating from a gymnasium[1] in N., Ira Sakavichanka, the daughter of a forest ranger, took up a position as a rural teacher in a remote province near Krupki, the estate of the Abdziralovich family. She was at a crossroads: she wanted to take advanced courses, help her parents teach younger children, work, and earn money. She wanted — just like that, for no apparent reason — to hide away in a

---

1. In many European countries, a gymnasium is a type of secondary school that prepares students for higher education. These schools focus on academic learning, covering a broad curriculum that includes languages, sciences, mathematics, and humanities. The gymnasium is traditionally seen as a more rigorous educational path, often leading to a final examination or diploma that qualifies graduates for university admission.

remote corner, at a poor school, teaching children, reading books, and pondering life's unexpected turns. She had been introduced to the Belarusian movement while still in school: the gymnasium students gave her Belarusian books to read. Before starting her job, Irachka thought like this: the revival would need highly educated people, so she would work at the school for a year or two, save money, and then go to study. She considered many options... But everything turned out differently.

She taught near Krupki for four years — until that memorable spring when she fell in love with student Abdziralovich. She later transferred to the Horki district, to be closer to Horki: many had told her that there were quite a few *sviadomy* Belarusians among the students in Horki agricultural educational institutions. She wanted to erase that spring from her memory, renounce all love, and devote herself wholly to "the only holy work – the work for the Belarusian revival." Having moved to the new school, she soon established contacts with Horki. There, during the first Belarusian theater play, she was deeply, pleasantly moved and disappointed at the same time. She saw the tremendous efforts of a handful of idealistic youths, how little had been done, and how much work still remained to be done everywhere. She immersed herself in this work as much as strength and time allowed. She sowed Belarusian consciousness among the peasants and peasant intelligentsia. She taught not only children but also adults to read, write, recite, and sing in Belarusian. She taught without Belarusian textbooks, as they were impossible to obtain from across the demarcation line.

This work captivated her. For a long time, Ira seemed to have no thoughts of that spring, that love, or those memories. She seemed to have forgotten about Abdziralovich.

But now, upon hearing that he was living in N., that his father wanted to reconcile with him, and that his lack of awareness could be detrimental to the cause, Ira lost her peace again, only she didn't dare to admit it to herself. She tried to think that she had never loved Abdziralovich, that what she had was something that couldn't even be called love... But then why did she think of him involuntarily? Why did memories of that spring flood back? Why did she long to lie endlessly under an apple tree in a hammock made from an old master's haybag, quietly talking with eyes closed and arms weak from inexplicable fatigue?

And why would such gloomy thoughts be creeping into her mind for the first time? Thoughts that she worked, worked tirelessly, but where was the joy of personal life? It only happened once, only with him. But she worked then, too, so why was that spring always a sunny, joyful celebration? And now? Would there never be personal happiness again? Years flew by, flew by... She no longer looked like she had in the photos taken at the N. photography studio that spring. The cheerful, joyful laughter in her girlish eyes had gone, that youthful freshness had faded. Her heart clenched with sadness, and she was ashamed of these thoughts! That was a betrayal of the holy cause. Could one hold back on strength, beauty, and youth for the revival of the Motherland?

She ran into the house, set the gramophone by the open window, and wound up the first record she could find.

And she felt ashamed that on a weekday when everyone was working with the sweat of their brow, harvesting and haymaking, she disturbed the rural silence with the sacrilegious, boisterous singing of the gramophone:

"Cook, cook the potatoes
from the oven,
In a bag and over the
shoulder..."

With a nervous, almost ridiculous motion, she flicked the needle away and listened to the sudden silence of an empty room ringing in her ears. She did not want to have lunch. She ran to the apple tree and lay in the hammock, face down on the pillow. She gradually calmed down as she swayed. The midday August sun gilded the leaves in the orchard, sneaking through its cover toward the swaying girl. A bee buzzed somewhere, and empty wheels rattled far away on the road. A leaf on an apple tree branch nodded, just like the edge of the scarf on her head as it rested on the pillow. She slept. She slept or maybe she didn't sleep — she heard everything, knew everything, as if sleeping, but unable to truly asleep...

Irachka thought her thoughts.

It was not in the hammock that she was rocking, but in her childhood cradle, just as she had done when she was little. Flies crawl closer, annoyingly clingy, even under the baby's mattress, making the air stuffier, and then grandmother-nanny, upon hearing movement, leans in and sings the wondrous tune of her childhood years:

"Go, kitty, to the forest,
Bring a belt for Ira...
Go, kitty, to the market,
Bring some raisins for the
girl...
Go, kitty, to the fair,
Bring a pie for the young
lady..."

The cradle squeaks quietly. The sunlight pierces through
the cover, stirring the swaddled little lady, and the nanny
sings the song that now emerges in Irachka's mind,
somewhat gloomy or sleepy:

"A kitty sat in the
kitchen,
Her little eyes swollen...
"Why do you cry, little
kitty:
Do you want some food or
drink?"
"Neither food nor drink I
want,
I cry out of my own
sorrow...
The cook licked the liver
away,
Blamed it on me, poor

kitty;
They want to cut off my
paws,
How will I walk then?.."'

Grandmother sings the song that she sang to her children, a sweet melody that she herself had listened to eighty years prior.

Irachka's thoughts wandered.

Why hadn't she gone to the fields to reap wheat with the women today? She would not have been so bored then!

With the dew and freshness of the early morning, reaping is pleasant and easy. But by day's end, the back aches. And it's embarrassing, too, to have your figure and backside on display. Swish, swish! The sickle whirs. Tiny bugs, beetles, and ladybugs scatter away. A gray mouse darts from under the stubble to its hole. You should have gone to harvest wheat with the women today, Irachka! You are daydreaming of who knows what under the sun, and your heart aches.

She tossed and turned like this until the evening, lying down, then running around, finding no peace. And when everything quieted down in the sleepy village, the melancholy moon glided across the blue sky, while some lonely, anxious clouds passed around it, stirring the sleeping garden with an uneasy breeze. Ira stepped out of the house, gazing at the crimson-black poppies in the garden, breathing in the scent of the blooming tobacco, and listening to the silence. After standing for a bit, she wandered around the garden, returned to the house, paced across her room, went to the empty classroom, walking there, gazing through the dim and shiny glass onto the bright moon crescent, and again retreated to her room, where the window had been left opened, carrying through it a cool breeze.

Her school was divided into two halves by a narrow corridor: in one there was a classroom, and in the other the teacher lived. The latter half was much smaller; it was a single room with a corner partitioned off by a thin wooden divider, where the teacher slept. Along one wall stood a long, large table, completely covered with books, sheet music, various papers, and gramophone records. Between the table and the window stood a wicker chair made of willow, with a high, reclining backrest, very comfortable when one is weary or daydreaming. A wide, soft sofa stood by the other wall, with a guitar draped in a red ribbon, and Belarusian-style armchairs — big, hard, and simply carved — at both ends.

On the walls bereft of wallpaper hung a small map of Belarus, and above it, framed and wrapped in a Belarusian sash, there was a small portrait of Yanka Kupala. On another wall, there were Turgenev[2] and several cutouts from illustrated magazines and photographs of Belarusian writers and notable figures, simply pasted onto paper. Two windows opened into the garden. One was always covered with house plants; at daytime, the other one revealed flower beds with beautiful, large flowers, several patches of vegetables, and beyond — a small orchard of a few apple and plum trees, bushes of currants and raspberries. The vegetable patches were lush with fine blooming poppies, with large, red petals

---

2. Ivan Sergeyevich Turgenev was a Russian novelist, short story writer, and playwright, considered one of the greatest authors of the 19th century.

and several pods, already quite sizeable. A mustachioed, curly pea meandered next to it, holding on to tall, knotty stakes with its weak coiled tendrils, beginning to bloom with tiny white-violet flowers. In the flower beds, there grew tobacco, marigolds, fragrant peas, and several other blossoms. Both the flower beds and the vegetable patches had grown rich and dense, as though wild; they did not get careful daily tending and were thriving all on their own.

Once again, the dreary crescent moon and the quiet, sleepy garden lured her out of her cramped room toward where peas thrived and poppies blackened in the darkness. But for how long? After standing there hopelessly amid the beautiful yet joyless whispers of the tortuous night, she ran back to the confinement of her small room.

Walking along a narrow path overgrown with low, trampled pampas grass and nameless knotweed, Ira plucked a red, curved poppy petal with a black spot in the middle, tearing it mindlessly and bringing it to her lips. When she arrived, she wound up the gramophone, put on 'The Spring Tale,' sat in the wicker chair, leaning back, and closed her eyes. Fresh and clear like spring itself, sounds of the violin poured out from the gramophone horn, but despite this, the girl recited from Kanstantsiya Buylo:

> "I will bury my love deep
> in my soul,
> Wear the calm of the
> Sphinx on my face,
> And though my heart may
> wither in pain,

I will not say a word to

you..."

She would stop the gramophone, go to the window, sit down, and look out at the moonlit garden, resting her chin on her hands.

XVIII

S ukhavey and Mikola Kantsavy were arrested and sent to the N. "extraordinary commission" — this was the news that was brought to the teacher by Khaim the Peddler a few days later. The girl was shocked but realized that there was no time to waste and hurried to Horki. She was certain that the letter had also fallen into the hands of the "extraordinary commission," and although she didn't know what would come of it, she feared that the arrested might be accused of espionage because of the letter. The lads from Horki tried to calm her down, but they themselves had completely lost their assurance because they didn't know why their friends had been snatched, and feared that they, guiltless, might be executed. After meeting, they entrusted Iraida Auhenauna, as a woman and the least suspect, to head over to N., find out what they were being accused of, and plead for their release into the custody of the school board and the teachers' association.

No one brought up the old question of asking her also to talk to Abdziralovich about the letter and the money.

When Ira arrived in N. early in the morning, the late summer air was already palpable there. Ira was no longer accustomed to the city, but found pleasure in the hustle, the crowds, and the culture. She peered at the familiar sights seen long ago but was preoccupied with how to free the arrested.

Having rented a hotel room and quickly settled in, Ira stepped outside with some hesitation in her heart and hurried to the "extraordinary commission," determined to do everything she needed in one day.

The building that housed the feared Bolshevik institution was well known to the girl: it was an episcopal school before the war, and Ira had attended parties and dances there. Now, few people walked past that building, and those who did stayed in the middle of the street, as the building with its stone wall and sidewalk was fenced off and wrapped in barbed wire. When the teacher approached, a huge wagon stood at the gates, filled with soldiers' loaves of white bread, and soldiers were throwing the bread from the wagon onto the tarp on the ground. Ira didn't go there; she went to the porch, where two Red Guards with carbines stood on either side. They asked her for a pass, and when she showed her documents, the older soldier said that these papers were worth no more than "spit" to them and that she needed a pass from the city commandant. She thanked them and ran off to look for the commandant.

She asked many people where he lived, but no one knew who she was looking for. Others told her to go to the "*saviet*"[1] and the soldiers didn't know either. Then, a newspaper boy from whom she bought the paper told her that the commandant's office was across the bridge, near the station.

---

1. *Saviet* (bel.савет), town council.

A tram arrived soon afterward; she got onboard and went. And there, on the street near the commandant's building, there were a lot of soldiers and all kinds of people. They only let in those who were municipal officials or were known to the soldiers, and no one else. For a long time, Ira couldn't understand why she, some peasants, and some townspeople weren't allowed in, and no one knew anything, no matter whom she asked.

The doormen shouted:

"You'll have enough time, you'll have enough time, why are you pushing?"

But the line of those waiting kept growing, and soon nearly a dozen people stood behind Ira. None of this boded well, but she was firmly determined to remain calm and patient for the cause. A clerk came out and began handing out white tickets to those waiting, but not to everyone, because others surrounded him from the sides, shoving blue tickets in his face, and he gave them nothing.

By the time Ira made out that her white ticket had the next day's date scribbled next to a stamp, the clerk shouted:

"Blues — the reception... begins!"

And disappeared.

The blues rushed to the doors, pushing and shoving, and ignoring the armed soldiers, while the whites, as if guilty of something, stepped back in confusion and looked around. Ira stopped by a linden tree that had been gnawed by a horse, thinking about what to do, and some local man with an unwashed face, dark as a Semite but with good pronunciation, got close and whispered to her that they could swap their tickets. Ira was happy because it was already past noon, and the entire day could be lost.

She wanted to do the exchange but felt someone's intense gaze on her. She looked over and saw a fat man with a green, sickly face wearing the shabby coat of a clerk, whose eyes conveyed to her the same thing as the dark man had. Ira worried that she might get into some kind of trouble with this exchange — better to lose a whole day than risk it. When the dark man went over to the peasants, the shabby clerk approached her, squinted his pleading eyes, and said, pulling a blue ticket from his sleeve:

"Don't despise the hungry and give whatever your kindness allows..."

Ira exchanged her ticket and gave three Tsarist rubles to him. To avoid seeing how he bowed and how tears crept down his green face, she hurried past the people and soldiers into the office. Having gathered all the documents in her hand, she stood in a small queue in front of the clerk's desk and was horrified to see the end of another queue that stretched into a corridor, toward the closed door of a room with a sign that read: "Commandant." The first hour past noon had already passed, and Ira regretted not having exchanged tickets a little sooner.

She showed her papers to the clerk. He didn't take them and told her to return the following day, as the commandant wouldn't have enough time to see her today anyway.

With a timid but rather insistent voice, Ira asked:

"Is it impossible to get a pass without the Commandant?" and then added, more firmly, "all my documents are in order, here..."

She was the only one standing in front of the clerk. He read and examined her papers for a long time, then said to her:

"So what do you want from us, Comrade? We don't issue passes to the "extraordinary commission". The council does. If you want to buy shoes, you surely don't look for them in a pharmacy... I just don't understand what you want..."

"I am sorry! I was sent to you for a pass from the "extraordinary commission". I didn't make it up myself..."

"Don't argue, Comrade!! They couldn't have sent you to us, because we haven't issued passes to the "extraordinary commission" for almost a month already. Do you understand that or not?"

"I understand... Just tell me, please, who is issuing them now?"

"The council, obviously... Find the commandant of the town council building — Karl Marx Street, the former "Belarusian Hotel". Any fool can show you the way!"

"Ah... thank you!"

Sweating, Ira ran out into the street and was glad to have dealt with that clerk and glad that everything was calm outside. Peasants sat under the fence with patient indifference, while soldiers sat on a bench cracking sunflower seeds. Withered yellow leaves fell onto the broken brick sidewalk from the horse-nibbled linden tree.

The town council was nearby, and Ira hoped she'd manage to get an entry pass for the "extraordinary commission" before two o'clock, even if it would be for the following day.

At the council, they let her pass through the doors quickly, and she hurried up the stairs to Room No. 3, where the general office was located, and where the clerk on duty received the public. However, a large crowd of people stood waiting near this room, and Ira, exhausted and irritated, leaned against the wall. She lost all hope of accomplishing anything that day and regretted the time wasted in vain. She picked up a newspaper to calm herself and collect her thoughts until her number was called. Her eyes carelessly wandered over the newspaper lines, and a myriad of thoughts crowded her mind, but she couldn't grasp the one, most important thought: *Why am I so hasty? I'll manage this in time; I need to be more patient...*

"Good day!" she heard a voice beside her and raised her eyes.

"Ah!.. Good day... I didn't recognize you," quite calm on the outside, but completely flustered on the inside, the teacher looked at Abdziralovich and quickly extended her hand to him, forgetting herself. He gently and cordially shook her hand, and the girl felt a pleasantness from his touch. He wore an overcoat without epaulets and a cap without a cockade, the spot where it had been was darker than the surrounding material. He had matured considerably. His brown eyes had aged, and small wrinkles that she had never seen before appeared under his eyes, at the sides. He did not shave his mustache but only trimmed it. If it weren't for that same gentle voice, she would not have recognized him right away, or he would have seemed more foreign to her.

Somehow, without thinking, they moved away from the line of people toward the window. He didn't ask her why she was there but inquired about the number on her ticket. Seeing that it was number 315, he said that there was no use in continuing to wait today because they would only see people up to number 300, — according to what had been told to him by a clerk he knew, whom he'd called out from the office through the doorman. Her face betrayed such dissatisfaction, such disappointment, that he thought she had come here due to some misfortune, in search of salvation. He wanted to ask but again remained silent.

They exited the council and walked down the street toward the boulevard.

"If you, Iraida Auhenauna, don't have any acquaintances in this new bureaucratic machine, then you'll wait in vain in all kinds of queues for a very long time," Abdziralovich said.

"No, I don't know anyone, or maybe I do, but I don't know it, since I only arrived here today. I need a pass to the "extraordinary commission" to inquire about the arrested... one of whom you know all too well."

"Who is that?!"

"A teacher, a *sviadomy* Belarusian, Mikola Kantsavy."

"He's in the 'extraordinary commission'?!"

"Yes, exactly."

"My God! Mikola, good, honorable Mikola in the N. "extraordinary commission." What a tragedy! Or is it a mistake? He must be rescued! For what, what was the reason? Iraida Auhenauna tell me?"

"How would I know?" she replied with a question. "They came, thoroughly searched everything, took all the correspondence, some Belarusian books, arrested him, and with him one student from Horki, another *sviadomy* Belarusian, Sukhavey."

"For what?"

"None of us knows... We fear they'll accuse them of counter-revolutionary activities for their Belarusian work and execute them."

"Oh, God save them, that can't be; you're unfairly harsh in your thoughts about the Bolsheviks. They can't kill the innocent!"

The girl didn't respond, and they walked through half of the park alley in silence. He noticed that she was upset, and very much wanted to stay with her longer and comfort her.

"Ignat Vosipavich!" Ira looked at him with her round, gray-blue eyes. "Let's not delve into criticisms of the Bolshevik regime... just do everything in your power to save our arrested, because God forbid anything happens... it would be such a loss, such a loss; if only you had any idea!" she nervously adjusted a bunch of hair near her ear and fell silent again.

"Well, yes, of course," he said. "But please don't take everything to heart just yet; I think everything will be alright, and it's not as bad as it seems." He was trying to reassure the girl and remembered the nicer times when he and Kantsavy had studied together. "I will do everything in my power to free my dear Mikola and his friend, because you have no idea how much I value Kantsavy."

"You appreciate him as a generally good person. But I value him even more as an advocate for our homeland's revival. Losing him would be as painful for me as it was when my mother died."

"Ah, so... your mother died..."

He paused, thinking. Then he said:

"It's true, I can't feel it the same way... the pain from losing him as an advocate for the Belarusian cause... I couldn't. I didn't even know he played such a role in the 'movement'."

Abdziralovich felt an imperceptible sorrow dampen his joyful mood. The sorrow arose from the fact that she spoke so reverently about another, who was different from him. But he didn't want to see this as the reason, and so he searched for it in his disapproval of any kind of fanaticism.

"That's a pity..." she said.

"What's a pity? That I didn't know all of Mikola's qualities or that I am not made like someone who is able to feel everything..."

"All of it," she answered and picked up a yellow maple leaf from the path. "Well, it's good that you've learned to speak Belarusian," she said and warmly glanced at him with her round, gray eyes. "Before, it seemed, you spoke it with difficulty; either you didn't know it well... or didn't want to."

"Don't think, Iraida Auhenauna, that I'm such a bad Belarusian. Who knows? If I were in an openly Belarusian sphere, maybe I, too, would be doing some work that is beneficial for the *homeland*..."

He said the word "*homeland*" with slow emphasis as if mustering courage or with a hint of jest, defending his earlier inactivity.

"I even bought a Muscovite-Belarusian dictionary recently. Found it displayed in a shop window."

"Really?" she said softly, extending the vowels, with shy joy and a growing sense of delight, and she gazed right into the depths of his soul, so much so, that he felt an unfamiliar sweetness. "Well, then, here... I give you this maple leaf!" she added.

And with an unexpected awkwardness, she lowered her eyes to the path.

"Thank you," he murmured quietly and just as awkwardly.

"We were talking about parents..." she regained her composure. "Forgive me, Ignat Vosipavich..." she raised her eyes. "That I didn't tell you right away. I didn't know what would be better: to tell you or to wait... In Sukhavey's possession there was a letter for you from your father. A student from Horki had brought it from beyond the demarcation line. The letter's whereabouts are unknown right now... Your father is ill; he's calling for you."

"My God! So many surprises and so much news today..." he said and involuntarily covered his face with his hands.

She glanced at him silently and trembled with invisible joy.

XIX

The unexpected news, however, did not end there. As sometimes happens in life, it continued pouring down on him even in the days that followed, as if this streak had been destined for him.

At the "extraordinary commission", he learned that Kantsavy and Sukhavey had been charged with spreading counter-revolutionary propaganda among the peasants, which was harmful to Bolshevik authorities. They would not be released into the custody of the teachers' council or the school board; resolutions from the Committees for the Poor would be needed for their release. He was told he could only see them on Saturday, and only in the presence of the guards.

He hurried to Ira and relayed all this in gentler words to the despairing girl. While waiting for her response, he informed her that he had decided to visit Harshchok that evening to ask for advice and help. He hoped that they would go to the garden before the evening, that she would agree to walk with him, and that even someone like her would need a little stroll in the fresh air to get away from all these distressing thoughts. He hoped that the sadness of these events would pass, that something as sweet as when she had gifted him a maple leaf in the garden would surely happen again, bringing them closer and fostering a much-desired loving friendship.

But the girl was upset for a long time, did not go to the garden with him, and only thought and talked about Saturday, wishing for it to come sooner so that she and Abdziralovich might go see the arrested. Ira was upset that freeing their friends would not be as easy as it had seemed before; she suddenly felt so powerless from the lack of hope. She was so sad and hurt that she reproached herself for her normally cheerful disposition, which had now abandoned her. She sensed an unpleasant discord in her relationship with Abdziralovich.

Having left the hotel, Abdziralovich did not know what to do with himself until the evening; he felt weariness and emptiness in his mood. He crossed to the other side of the street and, having gotten lost in thought, involuntarily stopped. He raised his head and looked at the second-floor window of the hotel, where her room was. When he thought he saw something move by the window, he became embarrassed and hurried down the street toward Vasil's place.

Vasil was at home. He had just returned from a work trip, and was lying on the bed in his boots, resting. He looked tired, thinner, and somewhat pitiful to Abdziralovich.

Rather quietly, he welcomed the guest and apologized for lying down.

"Maybe you want some tea?" he asked.

"And you?" replied the other.

"I want some," said Vasil, got up slowly like an old man, went to see the landlady, and then sat down on the sofa, looking more cheerful.

"I got so exhausted on the trip, you have no idea," he said, looking somewhere past his guest.

"Did you requisition the grain from the peasants?"

"Requisitioned..."

They sat in silence for a long time, each lost in his own thoughts.

"Tell me, Vasil, about the village," Abdziralovich asked. "How do the peasants take to the requisitioning?"

"How do they take to it?" Vasil smiled crookedly. "Well, so-so, here and there; sometimes with clubs, sometimes by other means..."

Once again, both fell silent, each reflecting on the village in his own way.

Abdziralovich was thinking that the village needed to be educated, that only then would his memories of how he had once run away from home out into the hayfield, shared a meal with the haymakers under a hazel shrub, and rolled in the fragrant, slightly wilted cut grass, that only then would his memories not be upset by anything: not the way little Taukach showed the finger to the portraits of the gentry, nor the fact that the committees might not issue the needed verdicts to Mikola and Sukhavey, which would be really, unexpectedly bad... The village needed to be enlightened.

Vasil was thinking that if they send him out again, he would ask that not just the brave Red Army soldiers accompany them, but some good advocates also.

Both were lost in thought for a long time.

Village... Countryside...

How I love it, but with a strange kind of love — one best expressed by the proverb: "too lonely when apart, too cramped when together".

With painful sensitivity, I cannot bear it when they scold and curse it for its backwardness, mocking its ignorance and stupidity. But in the depths of my soul, when its shameful images float joylessly in my memories, I myself despise and mock it without mercy, storing everything in my sickly heart.

I love and hate it at the same time.

It always happens that not even a month passes after I leave it, unloved, for the noise of city life, and already I want to forgive it everything, and already I feel sad that here, in the city, they talk so little of it and write so little, as though it is far away, somewhere far beyond the ocean.

Whenever I see how the city proletariat crowds cinemas and theaters during the time of leisure, hurries to libraries and reading rooms, hangs out at meetings and assemblies, always noisily discussing their rights and defending their interests firmly and without compromise, my thoughts fly to the tiny, remote Belarusian village. And feelings of envy toward the city, and of contempt for the village, and of ache for it, and of shame for it overwhelm, oppress, and torment me.

Like a murderer drawn to the scene of the crime, some unyielding force pulls me on each fair day to the city market "to marvel at the village." What does it look like now, under the Bolshevik way of our miserable life?

Pale, emaciated city riffraff and thin, gaunt women in worn-out city clothes huddle around the peasants' carts;

with begging, distressed tones and barely contained anger, they say:

"Uncle! My dear! Is there not a little bit of bread left from the road?"

"No bread," the peasant answers indifferently, without even looking. "Well, maybe for tobacco..." he adds anyway, looking disinterested.

And waits for a long while, patiently, in the filthy town square under the mottled, foggy, misty autumn sky, to see if anyone will swap with him for tobacco.

"Ah, it's come to this: neither bread nor tobacco," he reflects aloud. "You can't get anything with money anymore."

And upon learning that a newspaper now costs not five, as it once did, but thirty-five kopecks, he disinterestedly turns away from the newspaper boy and once again waits with patience as dull as the autumn sky.

And he has absolutely no concern for anything in the world. Let whoever wants to rule and reign do so, as long as he can just manage to get some tobacco and sneak it home so shrewdly that even the neighbor doesn't find out and doesn't come to borrow a speck of it.

And only for a brief moment does he liven up and stretch forward, leaving his cart behind, when Red Army soldiers scatter from their vehicle the free leaflets that had been sent to the market by the propaganda department from their expedition.

And I'm not so upset anymore that one won't see any lively images of the village on the pages of the Bolshevik city press: if one did, the cheeks of its impartial defenders would be flushing with shame.

Oh! Dark and poor are our houses.

Miserable is the appearance of our homes.

And miserable is the spiritual life of their inhabitants.

Even in the moments of the greatest upheavals of life and the most significant shifts.

Even in this swirling whirlpool, in this roaring volcano of revolutionary events.

When they have something to eat in the village, they will eat it with dirt and dust. They will scatter it on the table, soil their chests, and dirty their fingers, as though smeared with wheel grease. They will eat the gifts of nature just the way they come from the ground: with soil, with husks.

If they have something to sew clothing from, they sew it so that a chimney sweep would wear it! Poorly and awkwardly, sometimes too long, sometimes too short, very crooked, and very skewed; just like the "grays" from Mscislaŭ ridicule the "whites" from Horki: *holy terror on pitchforks.*

A miserable life, and a monotonous life. There are no books here, there is no art. There are card games and spiteful, detestable thoughts. There are no beautiful experiences. There are no tempting feelings or courageous revolutionary aspirations. And even if the very beginnings of them can be found in one's youth, they are soiled by dirt all too quickly. What remains is cursing, swearing, and anger.

"So, to tell you about the village," Vasil perked up. "When I was on this trip, I ended up at a meeting in a village in Pyatrovicy district near Mscislaŭ. Nowadays, it's mostly the youth who attend these meetings, the elderly would eat them alive if they could. Well, when the matter is important, then the elderly also come to shout and argue with the youth."

"There's this one man of around fifty years old, with a big beard, shouting: 'Brothers! What kind of freedom is this when there's no tobacco... It's available in town, but they don't sell it; they want a pound of flour for an eighth-pound of tobacco. I sent my son,' - and his son is about twenty-five, - 'but he has been on the front lines, has become lazy, and won't go...'

And another man asks: 'On which front lines?'

'Somewhere in Kirpaty.'

'Ah, yes, yes! My son's the same. Doesn't want his father to smoke tobacco, afraid there won't be enough bread till the new harvest. But I tell him: *What's it to you?* And I start scolding him. I grabbed a knife to scare him, and he got quiet. And afterward, he said: *That's not true, when Lenin gets healthy again, you, old men, won't have such luxury anymore...* And I told him: *No, you, damned ones, will die of starvation with your self-governance.* And he replies: *Why would you, the old, not be healthy; you went barefoot until you were twenty and didn't cut your hair, while I, from eighteen onward, hauled carts for contractor Lyavonau in Moscow, and then for three years sat in Kirpaty for Mikalay Kravazherny[1], in the trenches, sometimes not eating for three days and nights.* I tell him: *Leave! Leave my house, go wherever you want!...* And truly, he listened to his father: took his hat and left.'

Here all the elders applaud: 'You're a good man! Such bandits need to be taught a lesson!'

---

1. *Kravazherny* (bel. краважэрны), bloodthirsty, referring to Tsar Nicholas II of Russia.

And another man adds: 'Even as Abraham carried his son to God to sacrifice him on the altar, his son Isaac remained silent...'

And everyone then agrees: 'True! True!'

Then the most respected and wise man steps up and says this: 'And mine, son of a b..., had gotten a hold of some books on politics and keeps reading: everything belongs to the people, you cannot sell bread if you have a little surplus. My wife denounces me for swapping five pounds of flour for five eighth-pounds of tobacco in Pyatrovicy town. Then I say: *What's it to you? I am the master here...*And whack her. Then my son ran over protesting: *You have no right to hit her!* And I tell them: *Get out of my house! What do you mean I have no right to hit my own wife?'*

Oh, here the elders burst out laughing: 'Ha-ha-ha!'

A young man steps forward and says: 'Comrades, quiet! Enough fooling around. We have serious matters to decide: how do we open a school?'

But no one listens, everyone's talking nonsense...

Another young man comes out and says: 'Comrades! We need to open a school for sure. There are no schools in three villages, in both Shkandziny and Harelautsy. And there is not a single educated person among us, Comrades, we are all ignorant...'

The wisest man shouts at him in protest: 'Don't listen to him! He only just learned to blab with his mouth... The lumber may be free, but he didn't mention anything about the taxes once we open the school.'

And another man says: 'They decided to charge forty rubles for a load of firewood — go, enjoy your life now...'

And someone else yells out at the top of his lungs: 'I have no one to send to school!!'

'What about your son and daughter?' - asks the young man.

'Then who will weave my *lapti*[2] for me?' - the man shouts.

'You, yourself?' - the young man asks again.

'Me? I've woven enough in my forty years!'

And the elderly decide: 'No need for a school, no need. It will corrupt the children!'

Still another one mutters: 'The Anisaus got educated, now they tell their father to listen to the *saviety*. What *saviety*? These ones: every house has a *saviet*, a council... Council means the whole family, and every man should obey it, and the household council obeys the village council, the village obeys the district council, and so on. Ah! shouted Anis, *I am the master of my household, and I will not obey you! You're not happy that I trade tobacco for bread — I have no needs for Tsars like these...'*

And another one responds in jest: 'It's alright, brothers, keep smoking! And if these hangmen don't notice, distill moonshine, too! And if there's no bread, let the Bolsheviks provide it. It's because of them that the factory closed; they don't distill spirits.'

---

2. *Lapti* are bast shoes made primarily from bast, fiber taken from the bark of trees such as linder.

A member of *kambed*[3] comes forward and says: 'No, Comrades, whoever distills moonshine should not ask for bread, but will be shot!'

As soon as he says this, all the elders roar: 'Ah! So they'll shoot us if there's not enough bread! Oh, save yourselves! We don't need leaders like these, no!'"

Vasil fell silent for a moment, as he had gotten excited and wanted to share more. He glanced at Abdziralovich to see if he was listening attentively to his stories and noticed that the guest seemed interested, but also preoccupied with his own thoughts. It was unclear to him whether Abdziralovich was actually looking at him or lost in thought and looking past.

Abdziralovich averted his eyes. He hadn't been listening as attentively toward the end. He was looking closely at Vasil and seeking out resemblances with old lord Abdziralovich. He found more and more similarities in appearance and felt an inexplicable dread.

Vasil wanted to speak and so he carried on. He shared about how, at the meeting, they discussed the proposition put forth by the youth to open a cooperative store, similar to the one owned by Jews in Pyatrovicy town. The proposal was rejected by the elders, who thought that the young would place their own comrades in the store; the elders would devour them alive if they could. He described how the elders shouted: *Aha! And where will the money for the store come*

---

3. *Kambed* (bel.) or *Kombed* (rus.), abbreviation for Committees of Poor Peasants, were established by the Bolshevik authorities in 1918 as local institutions bringing together impoverished peasants to advance government policy.

from? Let it burn! No need for a store, no need, no need!! Let's go home, brothers! Vasil spoke, while his guest gazed at him, and then, as not to lose this train of thought, and to continue to listen and think his own thoughts, Abdziralovich asked:

"Is it really just the elders who are to blame? I heard from many that it's the opposite these days; the youth ride on the necks of the elders, as much as they please..."

He said this, while thinking that Vasil's nose resembled that of his father, old lord Abdziralovich, and that if the old man saw this son of his now and listened to him, what would happen then... What would happen if he found out that this Bolshevik, this worker was his own son.

"It's not just the elders who are to blame," answered Vasil. "There are good reasons to scold the youth too. But ideologically, undoubtedly, the elders are worthless, and truth is on the side of the youth..."

He got quiet, thinking, then spoke again.

"Perhaps, indeed, Ignat Vosipavich, I might seem to be biased to you, so let me say a few more words to show that there is scum among the youth as well. A poor Jewish blacksmith gave me a lift; he was heading to P. district for iron. He's a supporter of the communist order, but he told me so much about the youth in his village that they all ought to be hanged. The village is poor, so all the youth used to go off to the cities, but now they've returned home as slackers and bandits, and under the banner of Bolshevism, they mock all the peasants. They live as parasites, they have wormed their way into the Committee for the Poor, and no one can touch them. The chairman of the *kambed*, a rather young lad, was convicted of murder in Moscow; this summer he beat the wife of his brother, a farmer, with rakes so badly that she suffered for several days and died. So, he had his brother put away in "extraordinary commission" for alleged counter-revolutionary activities, and he beats his father daily with anything he can find, hitting him on the head, forcing the old man to work, while he himself drinks and carouses with his gang...

"In some regions the peasants have revolted..." Abdziralovich interjected, half-asking.

"Well, of course, there have been revolts..." Vasil replied in the same tone, flustered, his lips curling in anger and his cheeks flushed from the conversation. He then said: "What's worse is that they assign the task of suppressing the revolts and punishing the rebels to such bloodsucking beasts as the various drunkards from former officers, like all these Hareliks..."

After speaking with such anger, Vasil suddenly realized that his guest was a former officer himself. He felt his cheeks burning and glanced sideways at Abdziralovich. His anger, however, did not subside.

"What? Who is this Harelik?" the guest asked calmly.

"Some drunkard of a captain, maybe even a former gendarme. He ingratiated himself with our Karpavich and taught him to drink. They were sent to suppress the revolt, and they... they mercilessly shot entirely innocent people, ignorant villagers."

"What are you saying?!" Abdziralovich asked, his voice sounded disturbed but lacked the necessary emotion, and he faulted himself for it.

Vasil was greatly upset but tried not to show it.

The landlady knocked at the door and entered with a samovar. She was a stout, gray-haired woman in a greasy blouse and slippers

"I came to ask you to take me to Karpavich," said Abdziralovich to Vasil, after she had set everything on the table and left. "I'm going to request his help in freeing my arrested comrade and another person from the 'extraordinary commission.'"

"Alright, let's go," Vasil replied shortly, pouring himself tea. "As soon as we finish drinking tea."

Their moods shifted. Vasil no longer felt weary and dejected; he was burning with the need for action, creativity, and fighting for something. He burned his mouth with the tea and, without thinking, ate an entire piece of sugar. His cheeks continued to burn, and his eyebrows furrowed.

Abdziralovich felt a sense of relief regarding Ira, as if he had been reassured of some joy and felt entitled to say, "Eh, who needs that!" But what it was that was unneeded, whether it was the Belarusian national revival or his friendship with the girl, he didn't fully know and did not try to understand. It seemed these two circumstances only hindered the possibility of permanently preventing the execution of innocent people.

XX

Operating under the alias Harelik, Captain Hareszka worked among the Bolsheviks in the town of N. as a secret agent for the grand Moscow circle, "The Liberation of Russia". The circle aimed to revive the "one and indivisible" Russian Empire and dispatched its agents across all the former parts of the empire. Captain Hareszka, a Belarusian by origin, was sent to work in Belarus with significant sums of money and important missions of the most secret nature. Among other things, he was tasked with finding people suitable for organizing a peasant uprising and infiltrating the Red Army, earning the trust of Bolshevik leaders to be sent to suppress the revolt and crush it with extraordinary and frenzied brutality. He was also tasked with smuggling out of Moscow, as soon as possible, across the Western Front to beyond the Soviet territory, a certain high-ranking clergyman, an important member of the "Liberation" circle (the same one who had once been an Archimandrite at the monastery where Harshchok sought refuge, who had sold a precious pectoral cross of considerable historical significance), and to evacuate also two of his main associates, the monks Paisiy and Nikadzim.

When Abdziralovich and Vasil arrived at Karpavich's that evening, they found many Bolshevik commissars, enveloped in thick tobacco smoke, either as guests or meeting participants. But soon enough everyone dispersed except for one, seemingly a close friend of Harshchok. This was a tall man in a black leather coat and big boots; he was not yet old, but with a thick beard and a head of graying hair that appeared as though encased into a pair of large black glasses.

"Comrade Harelik!" said Harshchok, limping by the table. "We worked hard today, too hard... I think we have the right to *indulge* this evening, right?"

"I think so too; we should *indulge*," the man replied in a voice that sounded all too familiar to Abdziralovich, and began to roll a cigarette, while sitting at the table close to the lamp but leaning away from it.

Goodness, could it be Captain Hareszka?! thought Abdziralovich and with unexpected timidity, inspected Harelik more closely, but the latter gave no indication of having recognized the former warrant officer.

Yes, it's him, it's him... Abdziralovich thought, looking at Harelik's ear and neck, clearly visible in the light of the lamp, *it's him, with his red, parched skin of a drunkard and womanizer, now growing his graying hair, it's him...* This was his first surprise.

"These, brother, are my old acquaintances," Harshchok gestured toward them, speaking to Harelik in his rough, but not unpleasant voice. "The first one, Comrade Vasil, is a good communist; the other, I don't know for sure, but seems like a decent man, only takes too long to make up his mind. Hey,

Mehmet[1]!" he shouted into the doorway of another, a darker room. "Bring dinner quick, whatever you have, so that you, so that..." he then turned and asked. "Or are you, Ignat... Ignat..."

"Vosipavich," prompted Vasil.

"I am bringing it now," responded Mehmet.

"Or are you, Ignat Vosipavich, still not done with establishing your self-identity? I told you: do not take too long, or you might be too late! Have you forgotten?" he glanced at Vasil from under his grey, curly hair and limped by the table. "Have you forgotten?"

"No, I have not forgotten, but I may have made up my mind..."

"A-a-ah, well, well, that's interesting!" exclaimed Karpavich.

Vasil looked up at him too, but Harelik remained indifferent, continuing to blow rings of smoke.

"As you see, I, as a Belarusian, am gradually finding myself with Belarusian national and social consciousness."

"I don't quite understand," said Harshchok with a barely noticeable smirk. "But why 'gradually'?"

"What's there to understand?" interjected Harelik. "Comrade appears to be an independent agent of yet another, it seems, entirely new formation – a Belarusian one. I know Ukrainian ones well, I shot them with my own hands when I was on the Southern Front..."

A brief silence fell as the atmosphere grew somewhat tense. Then, unexpectedly, Karpavich said:

---

1. In the original Belarusian text, the names Mehmet and Akhmet are used interchangeably when referring to Harshchok's manservant.

"Oh, I know about those independents, even the Belarusian ones. Two of them were brought to our "extraordinary commission" for counter-revolutionary propaganda. But I don't believe that Comrade Abdziralovich would be involved in the same thing as they are."

Karpavich limped, sat down at the table opposite him, and fixed his eyes on Abdziralovich. Abdziralovich didn't flinch and calmly said:

"Do you know their names? Maybe I came to you about this very matter, to seek help and advice."

"A-a-ah, I see," Harshchok replied evasively. "Maybe we can talk about that later, and now, don't refuse: what the soul has, it offers."

He invited his guests to dinner. Despite their attempts to decline, Vasil and Abdziralovich sat down to eat. Mehmet, a Tatar from Nesvizh and a former soldier, now a kind of a manservant or cook, brought out glasses and a bottle of cognac with the food. Abdziralovich, it seemed, had not had the chance to see, let alone drink spirits, for about a year. The conversation didn't flow initially, but Harelik and Harshchok pressed on with the drinking and chattered more cheerfully.

Oh, Abdziralovich heard many strange things from them, as they got drunk and began to spit out nonsense. He tried to flee from there several times, feeling as if something sticky and dreadful was clinging to him, and choking him as they both boasted, one after the other, of their service to the Revolution and the people they had killed. He saw how uncomfortable Vasil was, how he suffered, and he himself suffered too, but curiosity (for it was all new to him) lessened his anguish. He regretted finding himself here at such a bad time and lost hope of getting to the point of business with Karpavich and asking for help in freeing Mikola and his student friend. Karpavich sent Mehmet to the cinema or wherever he wanted, locked the doors and drew close the curtains. Then he brought more cognac and a jug of warm summer coffee, and overwhelmed the guests with drunken babble. Harelik was aiding him, as if in jest.

"Your self-identity is a poor one, brother," slurred Harshchok to Abdziralovich when he could barely speak. "Poor, my brother," he tapped his shoulder with his fist. "Because it's all aristocratic tricks, to turn us the pro... prolet... proletariat against each other. I know, you're a son of the gentry and you look at me, laughing, thinking: the man's as drunk as a pig, yet he's a Bolshevik. But I, my brother, drink not from joy, but from sorrow... Great sorrow! How many pro... prolet... proletarians have we lost, how much blood has been spilled, and still we haven't saved the re-vo-lu-ti-on from the gentry of the world, no, my brother, here's what I'll say to you... Pour me another, Harelik! I want to drink with this Beralu... Be-la-ru-sian. Long live incanal... incena-ra-cenal... in-ter-na-tion-alism! Long live!!"

"Long live!" shouted drunken Harelik. "Shout, or I'll shoot you for counter-revolution, go on!"

"Long live," said Abdziralovich, while Vasil fiddled with a can of conserves, trying not to listen to them, already deeply upset.

"Well, Comrade, let's toast to your independent language and... to *God-created beauty*, or something... Not to the beauty of your language, no, because it, Comrade, is still poorly polished and uncultured, but to *living*,

God-created beauty, to girls, or something..." Harelik babbled to Abdziralovich, as though he was so drunk that he couldn't understand anything anymore. But having emphasized certain words, as if to awaken within his interlocutor old memories only known to the two of them, he looked into Abdziralovich's eyes in such a way that the latter understood as clearly as though he had spoken the words: *I recognized you, and you recognized me. And it's not surprising. But what is surprising, is where we meet? And what will come of all this? Right?*

And he didn't stop there but began to recount to Abdziralovich why Karpavich has a limp, as if he didn't know already. He painted a picture of how he had wounded Karpavich. Karpavich interrupted him with a drunken tongue:

"Don't tell him, Comrade Harelik, don't tell him, do you hear, come on? He knows about it better than you. He's an old acquaintance of mine, and you only heard about it from me, do you hear? He was there himself!"

But the captain didn't stop there and instead began to recount to Abdziralovich how they had suppressed a peasant revolt.

"They bring them to me into the headquarters. 'Revolted?' – 'Revolted.' – 'To the wall.' They undress them, lead them to another room – we hear: bang! They fall and hit their heads. And so one after another, the twentieth, the thirtieth. There were two brothers, *papovichy*[2] , left-wing socialist

---

2. *Papovichy (bel.)* or *popovichi (rus.)* are individuals belonging to the clergy, priests and their families.

revolutionaries. Supported the leaders. One of them almost faints, white as chalk, legs giving out, teeth chattering, can't say a word, stuttering. But the other one... another round, Karpavich, what do you say? — While the other brother, a great lad, stands calmly, holding his head high, though he knows he'll be undressed next. They bring him up. 'Revolted?' – 'Fought against oppressors.' – 'Want to be shot?' – 'Yes!' – 'Ah! A brave one! Well, get undressed.' He unbuttons his shirt. 'Kostik! Be brave!' – he says to his brother. 'Do you have any requests? Make it now,' – I say. 'I want to write a note to my mother.' – 'Write it. Take the younger one away.' The younger one fainted; they dragged him away, and this one shouts: 'Farewell, Kostik! I'm writing to Mother.' And he clings to a piece of paper, writing, but his hand, to be honest, is shaking: 'Dear Mommy! Don't cry – it must be so. They took Kostik away... A gunshot. He fell. That's him. Now it's my turn. Kisses.' Didn't finish writing. I grabbed my gun and shot him in the forehead. A brave lad, wasn't he?"

Abdziralovich listened as if mesmerized by something foul and disgusting, as if something sticky and dreadful was clinging to him, constricting his throat.

Harshchok drank, his eyes cast down to the floor.

"Well, it's time for me to head home, I can't take any more, I need to rest," said Vasil with undisguised dismay and stood up.

"Don't take this to heart, Vasilyok," drunken Harshchok tried to joke with him.

Vasil looked at him the way a disappointed student looks at a teacher he has surpassed, and said bitterly:

"Well, there's no pride in having killed more innocents than the guilty."

He and Abdziralovich began to get dressed.

"Am I not heading the same way with the Comrades?" Harelik turned more to Abdziralovich and stood up from the table on his shaky legs. His voice had a cynical calmness that was understandable to Abdziralovich; he appeared innocently calm, as if he understood nothing, and that's why Vasil's words clung to him the way peas cling to a wall[3].

"Ivan Karpavich! Please be so kind and help," with embittered ingratiation, but in great earnestness, Abdziralovich pleaded while on his way out. "Help free them from prison, because I swear to you, they were arrested by mistake, innocent of any charge against the Soviet authorities... Please, be so kind, don't forget..."

"Alright, alright... If that's the case, then I'll have them released now... alright, alright..." Harshchok muttered near the door, limping.

Outside on the street, Harelik asked Abdziralovich which way he was heading.

"This way? Oh, then I'm going with you, Comrade," he said. "What? And you're going that way?" he shouted mockingly at Vasil, who had already managed to move a little away from them. "And we're going this way... Goodbye, goodbye!" he shouted diligently, not just for himself but on behalf of Abdziralovich, and failed to notice that Vasil did not stop to shake their hands in a farewell.

---

3. Clinging like peas to a wall is a Belarusian idiom, meaning to bounce right off something without sticking.

When the sound of footsteps on the pavement had faded in the distance, Harelik looked around the sleeping street, deserted in the drowsy gleam of the moon in its third quarter, unapologetically grabbed Abdziralovich by the arm, and talked quietly in the fresh, brisk air of early autumn:

"Well, sir, had I known I would meet you here, I would have brought greetings from Alexandra Mikhailauna and the prince..."

Upon hearing these words from the sobering captain, spoken so casually, Abdziralovich sensed an attempt to test the waters, but the words also contained an obvious mockery and a show of power by the stronger over the weaker. He thought about how to respond and remained silent. Then the captain continued to speak.

"Are you not curious to know, my sir, how your old acquaintance Alechka is doing?... Alechka - then, and now, truly, Princess Alexandra Mikhailauna Halszanskaya... A living, God-created beauty, as they say... what's that?"

"And how do you know about this?" Abdziralovich asked, surprising himself, although he started to feel quite offended and intended to rebuke the impudent captain.

"Well, my sir, I arrived from the Caucasus not so long ago. So, what interesting things should I relay to you? Mikola Martynavich, though I barely knew him and mostly heard of him through the prince, left with his family for Romania. Everyone left, except for Alechka, because the prince had married her. And she didn't even graduate from the gymnasium. Well, it's such a turbulent time. We reminisced about you with her. Yes... She said you were a good man and dear to her, but she didn't like your softness.

The prince introduced me to her. Now they both left there... to where the prince was sent by his superiors. Well, and you, quid pro quo, tell me, sir, about your adventures since then?"

"I work for the Soviet service, just like you, Comrade Harelik, but it seems you're in the military, while I'm in civil service."

"Yes... Of course, of course... What? You're going down this street? Very well, very well... So, you say you're not surprised about my friendship with your limping friend? Is that so?"

"I'm not saying anything, but to be honest, it was convincing, this ...masquerade of yours, or how should I call it, I am not sure."

"Yes... convincing, you say... Well, but, my sir, give me your honest word that you won't tell anyone, agreed?"

Abdziralovich did not say anything. They reached the building where he lived. The moon poured its sleepy light, and somewhere on the next street, around the corner, a night watchman rang his bell. Hareszka grabbed Abdziralovich by the coat, leaned in, and, emphasizing each word, stared right into his eyes:

"You will give me your honest word, sir, that you won't speak of this; but not like the one you gave in Moscow, remember?"

"I don't find it necessary to give you any kind of word... And so I won't give you any... And please be so kind and calm down a little," said Abdziralovich, pulling away from the stench of stale alcohol.

"Ah... So that's how it is! Well, alright."

Hareszka stood silently for a while, lost in thought.

"When can I see you at your apartment?" he asked.

"Anytime, when I return from work. Just not at night."

"Alright. Goodnight."

"Farewell."

They parted without shaking hands. Abdziralovich rang the doorbell, waited to be let in, and heard Hareszka's quick and broad gait slowly fade away. The sleepy moon crescent sunk lower in the twilight sky.

XXI

On the Eastern Front, the Red Army decisively defeated the White Army. For this reason, the Bolsheviks in the town of N. declared a holiday on Saturday. Poor Ira Sakavichanka couldn't visit her friends in prison on that day, as everything everywhere was closed for the celebration. She had to wait another whole seven days... After consulting with Abdziralovich, she decided to use this time to travel to the village where Kantsavy was a teacher, and obtain a paper from the village *kambed*, stating that the arrested was not an enemy to the Bolshevik authorities and that the committee would take responsibility for him until the trial. She also hoped to get a similar paper for Sukhavey in Horki.

Returning from Zarečča, where she had gone to arrange a carriage, Ira encountered Abdziralovich on the hotel staircase. Out on the streets, people were already on foot with songs and music, carrying banners, and the cacophony of various sounds reached the staircase. The girl wanted to run into her room to hide from everything as soon as possible. Her indifference upon meeting him stung and prodded at his already frazzled mood. He followed her without the kind of joy he desired and hoped for. He thought that she was silently blaming him for not helping her in freeing the arrested, and that was why she was acting this way with him. And he, in turn, began to blame her for such girlish thoughtlessness, with which she carelessly judged him, degrading the pleasant warmth of their relationship with all kinds of matters.

"Oh, God! I've completely exhausted myself over these past days, and all for nothing, absolutely nothing, oh!" exclaimed Ira, collapsing into a chair and burying her head in her hands.

"What do you mean, all for nothing?" he interjected without eagerness. "We did what we could."

They both remained silent for a while. Faint sounds drifted into the room from the street, an orchestra was playing there, and processions of people sang and marched by. The sounds of "The Internationale" reached them. Abdziralovich listened closely and wanted to go out into the street. She looked into the mirror and slowly pulled back: she had lost weight and seemed pale from the days of running around and all the worrying in this unfamiliar space. She was surprised at how much of her usual spirit and cheerfulness she had lost. She wanted to feel again, to feel everything she had felt when she spent an entire day pining in the hammock. But she couldn't. Here, he sat right in front of her, but was even more distant and foreign than before. *Oh, my God! A life has passed, there is no more strength, weariness has taken over.*

He liked the melody of "The Internationale," enjoyed the singing; the commotion in the street invigorated him and stirred a sense of liveliness.

He said to her:

"In spite of everything, I really like the music of 'The Internationale.'"

He felt a creeping sense of shame for having said "in spite of everything" and added:

"Beautiful music, isn't it?"

"Yes, beautiful..."

She wasn't sure how to interpret the words "in spite of everything," but she took them to mean his opposition to the bloody deeds of the Bolsheviks and, having thought about it, she deliberately said:

"The melody of "The Internationale" is beautiful, but so far it does not evoke in my soul any image of sorrow or joy of any "international" community of people. I haven't seen and I don't know of such communities among nations on this earthly globe; for now, the melody of our Belarusian peasant Marseillaise speaks to me more, the melody that evokes in me the endless, thorny, bloody path to the *internationale* of my unfortunate people..."

After a pause, speaking a bit more calmly but with even greater sorrow in her voice, the girl continued:

"Indeed, with both melodies, I equally imagine the tragedy and absurdity for us, the reborn Belarusians, that strangers who are unaware that they have not yet shed their own national self-absorption, have come to us with "internationalism" only on their lips, with its fiction in their minds, and with fanatical mercilessness they undertook the task of turning the Belarusian nation into mere manure for the cultivation of their international fiction. Oh, may they be damned!" she exclaimed, with grief in her voice. "They want to make the marks of their own nationalism into internationalism for us. Well, thanks for the favor... Perhaps we can enter the international as equals with everyone, without this additional form of development!"

"Iraida Auhenauna! Why take everything so close to heart? It seems to me that all the misfortune here is from the dissonance between theory and practice. Please tell me: does the theory of communism allow Moscow or any other communists to forcibly *muscovize* Belarusians? Is the theory of internationalism to blame for Belarusian people being governed by Bolshevik commissars of all nationalities, except Belarusian? Or is it to blame for our famous Obliskomzap[1] having Armenians, Latvians, Jews, Poles, Muscovites, but not us, not Belarusians? That the province has only such lame Belarusians as Harshchok?"

"Shall we go have lunch?" Ira asked him.

He smiled, silenced, and replied that he would, with pleasure.

As they descended the stairs, Ira recited the beginning of the "Marseillaise":

"Since ancient times
we slept, and were
awakened,
Told that we must act,
That man needs freedom,
needs land,

---

1. In Russian: «Областной Исполнительный Комитет Западной Армии и Фронта», meaning Regional Executive Committee of Western Army and Front, abbreviated as Obl-is-kom-zap.

That we must defeat the
villains..."

Gradually letting go of her anger, she said:

"I consider as villains both those who give stones as stones instead of bread, as well as those who give stones under the guise of bread. And I would beat them equally, be they a dissonance between theory and practice, or just mere tyranny."

Irritation stung his mood again, even more painfully. *Quiet down already, he* thought of her. *You haven't heard what I heard last night at that damned Harshchok's place; you don't know what's happening in my soul, but you reproach me for who knows what deeds...*

She glanced at him from the side, thinking that he was, after all, handsome, then turned away, thinking: *It's easy for you to conjecture now, but where were you, a Belarusian soldier, when the Ukrainians organized their national military units, separating from the Muscovite army? Surely, you were busy conjecturing even then.*

Out on the street, she hurried to pass the crowds and ran into the diner, while he watched, listened, and thought: *I ended up a lord's son through mere circumstance, I am truly a son of this dark community and should like to lead it to happiness better than anyone.*

They parted after lunch. Ira didn't want him to see her off in the evening, but she firmly and earnestly pleaded for him to do everything possible for the release of Mikola and Sukhavey. She almost cried, saying that her heart was sinking as if in foreboding of something disastrous, and asked him to inform her immediately of any news or changes in the matter. On her part, she almost swore that she would manage everything within seven days and would send him a telegram as soon as she got the paper from the *kambed*. He nodded in agreement and reassured the girl. After saying goodbye, he felt a certain relief, having been so unnerved by all this.

He wandered the streets and parks for the entire day of the Bolshevik holiday, visited the city square, and listened to the speeches of orators from the tribune. The lame Harshchok was especially popular with the audience. He did not express any new or important thoughts, and only cursed the gentry and the monks who'd once tormented him, struck his chest and the railing with his fist, and shouted in a thin, squeaky voice. Even so, his speech was well received by the common folk, who applauded him eagerly.

Sitting on a park bench, Abdziralovich thought of Ira with mixed feelings of sadness, offense, and irritation, then thought of his courtship with Alechka. *For what softness of character was I unsuitable for her?* he pondered. *That I was unable to pull her out of the hated bourgeois circles with the strength of my love? No, it's good that nothing came of it and we parted ways. Both of us would be unhappy because something would be pulling us in opposite directions our entire lives. And this way, she found her safe haven in life by marrying the prince.* And then again, he thought of Ira, of her gray, round eyes, so intelligent, but already lacking that youthful freshness that Alechka still possessed. That bright face with strands of lustrous black hair stood before his eyes, and he felt neither pity nor offense toward her. Ira's voice, soft, rich and internal, vibrated in his ear, awakening sadness and irritation.

From time to time, he thought back to that evening at Harshchok's place, overwhelmed with anger toward the common people and Bolsheviks like Harshchok. As for Hareszka, there was something dull, heavy, and hateful, that couldn't yet burst out into ordinary anger and seemed to be waiting for a special runway to unleash itself.

XXII

Ira was not able to return within seven days, as the villagers were too busy with work to gather for a meeting. Meanwhile, a counter-revolutionary plot was uncovered in N., and several members of the bourgeoisie were sentenced to be executed.

The entrance to N. was restricted for an undisclosed period of time, so Ira, having heard rumours of executions, was unable to go there to defend her friends and grew increasingly anxious, overwhelmed by dark thoughts.

Most troubling of all, she knew nothing: Abdziralovich hadn't written.

Meanwhile, Abdziralovich visited the prison the following Saturday and spoke with Mikola and Sukhavey in the presence of a guard.

Mikola was extremely happy that Ignat had found him, while Sukhavey, seeing in Abdziralovich a renegade, remained unfriendly toward him. Mikola had lost a lot of weight, turned pale, grown a beard, and become tormented by the fear of execution, completely losing his spirit. Sukhavey was calm, weary, but firm.

"Nobody here knows anything about your father," he told Abdziralovich, implying more with his words. "*Knowledge* disappeared in the village, word of mouth, as it were..."

Abdziralovich understood that the letter had not fallen into the hands of the "extraordinary commission," and he thanked him with a particular warmth:

"I thank you sincerely... Very well, very well..."

"And the money?" asked the student.

"I don't know yet..." replied Abdziralovich.

"So you're still a renegade... I was mistaken again," Sukhavey snorted angrily, left them, and moved away from the grills to the bunks. He sat there and didn't approach again, no matter how much Mikola pleaded with him "to act human."

The Red Army guard listened attentively to their conversation, then offered a friendly smile and said:

"You talk like peasants, but you go against the people."

"And where are you from?" asked Kantsavy.

"From the S. district, maybe you've heard of it."

"Oh, we have! Comrade Sukhavey!" he called to the lad. "This man is from your area, brother."

The student did not respond.

"He's angry," said the guard. "A student from Horki, I recognize his uniform..."

The visit ended there. Abdziralovich tried to reassure his dear Mikola, but the man had little faith in his hesitant words.

After that day, events unfolded rapidly.

The biggest news in N. was the gruesome and mysterious death of the communist Harshchok, who was found stabbed in his apartment. A note in his handwriting stated that no one should be blamed for his death.

Nothing was printed in the newspapers, but rumors about the death of the "cripple" spread quickly among the people, growing more terrifying and fantastic with each retelling.

On the evening following the death, Hareszka came to Abdziralovich, sat opposite him at the table, lit a cigarette, and said:

"It was I who stabbed him to death."

"And what do you want from me?" Abdziralovich exclaimed, his eyes open wide, feeling his fingers going numb.

"I need you to listen to what I have to say."

"I'm listening..."

"I received orders to smuggle one old archpriest and his two monks out of Bolshevik-land as discreetly as possible. I managed to transfer them here from Moscow. All we needed were passes for the demarcation line. We weren't lucky. Someone reported us; they got detained, were beaten, and thrown into the "extraordinary commission." I was in the favor of the late Harshchok. I earned this favor with entire buckets of thick, seared, blackened blood of the rebels. Once, Harshchok invited me to come look at something pleasant. He took me to the "extraordinary commission," run by his friend, a Latvian, the son of a former steward of the Halszansky princes. We were led into a dark cellar, where we found only these three monks, as usually the arrested get sent to prison. Harshchok relayed to me loudly, so the monks could hear, the whole story of how they had once wronged him in the monastery. Then he spat in their faces, tortured them, and then we left. Last night...

or today, or whenever... I came to thank him for the favor and the pleasant spectacle. Having sent away Akhmet and locked the doors, I overpowered him, gagged him, tied him up, and dragged him to the cellar – you know... they build them under apartment buildings here... I brought down paper, ink. After scorching of his heels, he agreed to write everything I dictated: permissions to grant the passes and so on. Admittedly, he attempted to revolt: lunged at me with a nozzle and broke the quill against my forehead, trying to gouge out my eye... see the mark? But I easily subdued the rebel and reminded him how we suppressed the peasant uprising in certain districts. He confessed that he was a pathetic rebel. Then I brought some kindling chips and paper scraps, lit another candle, sat beside him on a stump, and, looking at the bound man as I am looking at you now, told him an interesting story from my brother's life that happened in Kronstadt, a city infamous for its red glory..."

"It was right after the Socialist Revolution. A comrade prostitute, my acquaintance, was invited by the red sailors to their ball. During the intermission, her escort invited her for tea and led her to the hold room. There lay a young, handsome midshipman, naked and nailed to the floor by his hands and feet, with a handful of wood chips burning on top of his bare chest and a kettle with water boiling for tea... As I recounted this, I tore the clothes off Harshchok's chest, piled the wood chips over his hairy body, added some torn paper, and said: *Well, now let's see if this fire looked good on the chest of my brother ...*"

The captain's face flushed with blood. His hand trembling, he tore off the end of a cigarette, and continued:

"At that moment, Harshchok fainted, and instead of burning him, I doused him with water, then dragged him upstairs to the room, laid him on the bed, and as not to let him suffer long, I slit his throat. He lay there in a pool of blood, short, with his crippled leg bend under him..."

Hareszka and Abdziralovich sat in silence for a long time. There was a knock at the door.

The captain calmly opened it and let in a panting Red Army soldier. He then collected his hat and said, waving at the soldier to speak after he does:

"Well, stay healthy, Comrade Abdziralovich! Maybe we'll meet again sometime. You're starting to Belarusianize, and I, to be honest, am now helping Halszansky, who is currently working among Belarusians, *over there*. I thank you deeply for listening so attentively. I feel more relieved, as though I were stained and have now cleansed myself with fresh water."

And he left.

"Comrade!" the new guest whispered urgently. "I've come to say that you must rescue both my friend and yours. That student from Horki fled the jail the day before yesterday when my comrade from the S. district was on guard, and now he's been arrested too. And your friend, who stayed behind, he'll be taken somewhere tonight; there's already an order out... Save them, as I don't know how..."

"My God! What can I do?!" Abdziralovich moaned instinctively, clutching his head in distress.

***

...That very evening, Ira saw Sukhavey off on a long journey beyond the demarcation line.

The student paced quickly and awkwardly, without stopping, from the corner to the door. While she packed something in a knapsack for him, he turned his reddened, bloodshot eyes to the portrait of Yanka Kupala, then to the window, behind which poppies were darkening and tobacco whitening, and spoke, gasping as if in a frenzy, stumbling and tripping over the chair with his dusty boots.

"What? You thought I would rely on the help of that renegade? We're yet to see how he will help our friend Kantsavy. What? He told you he has "two souls"?... And you defend him? How foolish! It's not "two souls," but... but..." the boy flailed his arms. "...It's moral decay, degradation, spinelessness... something repulsive and slimy to me. Such degenerates ruin our Motherland just like any foreign enemy might... Eh, trash... What? It's time? You are ready?"

She silently handed him the knapsack. He slung it over his shoulder, grabbed a small walking stick, swayed to the side, then back to her again.

"Well, stay healthy, my friend! Don't abandon the cause!"

He awkwardly extended his hand, but she grabbed him by the shoulders, pulled toward her, kissed him once, then again, and whispered through tears:

"No... no, brother, I won't give up..."

"Don't see me through, don't go out!" he shouted from the doorway. And she watched from the window as he disappeared among the apple trees at the border and amid the hemp into the darkness of that early autumn evening.

She sat in the wicker chair and wept bitterly, alone.

Fresh air flowed through the open window, carrying the scent of tobacco.

XXIII

That very night, Captain Hareszka safely left N. and headed toward the demarcation line, having temporarily lost any hope of freeing the monks from the "extraordinary commission."

And on the occasion of the tragic day, the town council organized a public funeral for the unfortunate, slain commissar. All teaching in educational institutions was prohibited; municipal employees were ordered to attend the funeral procession. And the day turned out to be a good one: sunny and warm.

Abdziralovich woke up very late but in a cheerful mood. Without having tea, he sat down to write a letter to Sakavichanka, sharing good news about their matter, wanting to run and deliver the message himself. He wasn't afraid of the order, and was curious to see the funeral. He did not talk to Vasil about Karpavich's death the day before. Somehow, he didn't dare to start the conversation, but wanted to know what Vasil thought.

Vasil was sad the day before, and there were many reasons for that.

But Abdziralovich woke up calm and even somewhat cheerful. He was surprised that yesterday he couldn't comprehend and think clearly, but today, as he looked around, there was nothing to comprehend: all was well... True, the image of blood-covered Hareszka still lingered before him, but it felt unreal, like a dream or something lost in a fog. This wasn't what mattered to him. What mattered was that the good, glorious Mikola would be released, and he was about to write to Sakavichanka about it.

Joy is felt more deeply after sorrow! It was so delightful to watch the sunny happiness of windowpanes and the golden columns of dust that danced away from them and down toward the floor. And how miserable it had been!

Just yesterday, he sat here, hearing such terrible things from the captain. And only yesterday, he ran with that breathless Red Army soldier, looking for a way to find help from Vasil. They found him near his apartment, on the street. Vasil stood under a tree, leaning against a partition, hiding in the darkness from the light of a lamp from someone's window. Lost in thought and solitary sadness, he was gazing up at the sky, at the stars. But brave Vasil!

He instantly abandoned his sadness and ran with them to the prison. Despite the late hour, he managed to get to the assistant warden of the prison, comrade Kirdyushka, and learned the truth. God bless Vasil! He pressed Kirdyushka so much that the latter didn't know how to get rid of them and reassured them that the arrested Kantsavy was no longer with the "extraordinary commission" but had been turned over to the N. revolutionary tribunal, meaning that his case was not so serious, and he probably wouldn't be put against the wall to be shot. He also said: *It is because that arrestee is not important that they are transferring him to the former detention house, and they might even release him before trial.*

Abdziralovich took out a box with letters, paper, and envelopes, same box where his St. George's Cross was also kept along with photographs of acquaintances and the colorful maple leaf that she had gifted him, still fresh. He picked it up, looked at it, thought about something, and kissed it. Then he pondered for a long time about how to address her in the letter. *Dear? Dearly respected? Or just simply scribble: Beloved Iranka! No, impossible, she'll be offended, she'll sense an insincerity and will take it as overly forward.*

Right at that moment, there was stomping in the hallway and someone banged on the door.

Abdziralovich thought it might be the tea, but he was mistaken: it was Vasil.

"Excuse the intrusion. Were you writing something?"

"Aye, a letter to that girl I told you about."

"Ah, please continue, I will not interrupt," said Vasil, sitting down at the table, looking even more grim than yesterday.

"No, I'll finish it later; now we need to go to the funeral."

"Whose cross is this? Yours? You never boasted about it. What did you get it for?"

"For nothing, really."

"But really, what for?"

"For reconnaissance. That's the kind of person I am: if I am sent somewhere, I'll go, but I never volunteer myself to go. So, it was for nothing, and yet they hailed me as a hero. But that, as they say, isn't heroism."

"That depends on who's judging..."

"Why so gloomy, Vasil, huh?"

"There's no reason to be cheerful when everything is just falsehood."

"Eh, is it worth taking to heart? I've become so numb during the war that I've gotten used to all sorts of falsehood," said Abdziralovich, realizing that he only felt numb now, having uttered these insincere words, and even then, not very much.

Vasil silently handed him today's newspaper, printed in red with black mourning borders. The letters blurred before his eyes, and the black borders appeared blue.

Abdziralovich skimmed a few lines and felt shame and annoyance because much of it was eloquent nonsense and mere lies about the communist activities of the deceased.

"Shall we go to the funeral?" Vasil asked quietly. "Haven't you had your breakfast yet? You slept through your samovar. Let's go over to have mine; I left it hot."

Abdziralovich stopped reading, dressed himself, and they left.

The joyous, warm sunlight flooded the streets, glittering on the sidewalks, tram rails, and house windows.

Shops and everything else were closed, as on a holiday; working people slowly emerged from buildings, gathering, chatting, and queuing up for the funeral, like soldiers on a parade. From Zarečča and Slabada, crowds of workers arrived, decorated with red ribbons on their chests; in groups, they stopped on the corner and read the funeral ceremony schedule posted on the wall: where and when to gather, and whence to join the procession.

A red battalion with a music orchestra was marching, a car with an oak wreath rushed by, and they were about to bring out the coffin.

Abdziralovich wanted to go in and see the deceased, but Vasil wouldn't go.

"I went," he said. "This is what's there: an honor guard standing, nothing else. Akhmet was crying, complaining that the coffin lid wouldn't fit properly because the bent leg was sticking up high."

When they arrived at Vasil's apartment and sat down to have tea, a child's cry erupted from the landlady's side.

"What do you want? What?" shouted the landlady's relative, a Polish refugee. "Don't scream, because I have nothing to give you, understand? Be quiet!"

Vasil blushed, grabbed a bread crust, cut a smaller piece, and rushed out.

Abdziralovich heard him meet the landlady at the door, and she seemed to both object and encourage him:

"What are you doing, sir? You can't do that, always giving away all your food to Yuzik... God knows, we're so embarrassed; we don't even know how to thank the good sir."

Abdziralovich heard her shuffling in her slippers, while Vasil hurried to the child.

The music reached them from the street, the drum beat heavily. The procession had already started from the apartment of the deceased. Abdziralovich opened the window and listened to the sad, solemn, and beautiful sounds of the funeral march.

A dark swarm of people with red banners and fierce slogans poured down the street. Far in the distance, an open coffin with the deceased floated on the shoulders of workers, followed by a hearse. The sounds of the march grew louder, gripping his soul with something heart-wrenchingly solemn and ominous.

1918-1919

About the Author

 Maksim Haretski (18 February 1893 – 10 February 1938) was a Belarusian prose writer, journalist, folklorist, lexicographer, and educator. He is recognized as the first Belarusian existentialist author. Haretski was actively involved in the Belarusian national revival movement and published under various pen names, including Maksim Biełarus and Kuźma Batura. Haretski's literary works explored themes of human existence and national identity.

Haretski served in the Russian Army during World War I, and was imprisoned multiple times by both Polish and Soviet authorities – themes that often appear in his works. Maksim Haretski was executed by Soviet NKVD in 1938.

Two Souls
Maksim Haretski

Translated by Olya Ianovskaia from the Belarusian original:
Дзве душы (1919)

Cover design by
Grunwald Publishing

This is a first edition published in 2024 by Grunwald
Publishing
P.O. 405, Minden, Ontario, Canada, K0M 2K0
grunwald.ca